BOLAN RAISED HIMSELF TO A CROUCH . . .

as the big man came running. He planted both heels solidly, and when the man came into range, he swung. His right fist, still holding the snubnosed revolver for grip and solidity, buried into the big man's guts. Bolan reached and gripped, tangling his left hand in the man's long hair, and jerked his head down as he rose in a single motion and drove his knee upwards into the blurred face.

Bolan's knee met the face and he felt the whole nose go and some upper teeth. He jerked the head up and lowered his knee and smacked them together again, felt the man sag, and as he went down, Bolan chopped the snubnose across the back of his head.

Oh God, thought Mack Bolan, I'm tired. I am shot to pieces and I've been drugged and slammed up against a brick wall and it seems I've walked halfway across Manhattan. If they came to take me now—*whoever* the hell they are—I couldn't even defend myself.

Through sheer effort of will, Bolan made himself roll over onto his hands and knees and crawl forward. He had the thug's gun, his fat wallet, and he was going through his pockets when he heard slow, deliberate footsteps approaching along the parking lot's concrete paving . . .

THE EXECUTIONER:
SICILIAN SLAUGHTER

by
Jim Peterson

PINNACLE BOOKS • NEW YORK CITY

THE EXECUTIONER: SICILIAN SLAUGHTER

Copyright © 1973 by Pinnacle Books, Inc.

A Pinnacle Books original, published for the first time anywhere.

First printing, June 1973

Printed in the United States of America

PINNACLE BOOKS, INC.
275 Madison Avenue, New York, N.Y. 10016

To all those fighting the battle with Mack Bolan.
May they survive to fight again!

SICILIAN SLAUGHTER

PROLOGUE

Besides panic, death, destruction, and total disorganization of local *mafiosi,* The Executioner left oceans of blood behind in Philadelphia, including too much of his own.

By the time he crossed the George Washington Bridge in "Wild Card" John Cavaretta's forty-thousand-dollar Maserati, Mack Bolan felt his strength and vitality at a dangerously low ebb.

He had gunshot wounds in the left leg, his face, and—most dangerous of all his wounds—Bolan still carried a slug in his side. With gently probing fingertips, he could *feel* the damned thing. The wounds in his leg and side still leaked red. Bolan had seen men die of shock, knew its symptoms intimately, and finally acknowledged to himself he must have help—fast.

As though his condition were not problem enough, he also sat behind the wheel of an automobile so distinctive and readily indentifiable the Maserati might as well have been painted Day-Glo orange.

The man from hell ground wasn't worried about the cops so much as the *Taliferi,* the New York City "Family" whose soldiers had invaded Don Stefano Angeletti's Philadelphia estate. The same people who'd sent "Wild Card" Cavaretta to Philly for the express purpose of eliminating Mack Bolan from the face of the earth.

But Johnny Cavaretta's headless body now lay in Don Stefano's basement, along with the bodies of almost thirty other dead soldiers, and the don's son had stupidly and treacherously gone off to the *Commissione* with the Wild Card's head in a sack, to sell it as Mack Bolan's and collect the $100,000 bounty that was the standing offer that had been put on The Executioner's head soon after Sgt. Mack Bolan, formerly of the United States Army, declared his personal war upon the Mafia.

Sergeant Bolan had been in Vietnam on his second tour of duty, a weapons specialist, incredibly adept at infiltrating VC and NVR lines for "taking out" high ranking officers, political commissars, spies, and double agents. His invariably successful missions earned him the title of The Executioner; then he was abruptly given emergency leave and sent home . . . to bury his mother, his father, and beautiful younger sister, and arrange for the care of his permanently maimed younger brother.

Mack Bolan's father—a steady, sensible, hard-working man—had one night suddenly gone totally berserk, gotten out his old Smith & Wesson revolver, killed his wife, Elsa, his seventeen-year-old daughter, Cindy, and shot his son, Johnny. Then he'd gone into the bedroom and killed himself.

Sgt. Mack Bolan could not live with it. He'd known his father too well. When he talked privately to Johnny, Mack discovered how right his feeling had been. The old man had fallen into the clutches of local Mafia shylockers—

loan sharks; and through illness, fell behind in his "vigorish," the fifty percent plus hike on his loan.

The local Mafia prostitute recruiter enticed Mack's sister, Cindy, into his call girl racket as a "way to help out the old man."

The old man discovered Cindy's activities and blew his stack. He left a dead wife and daughter, a crippled son, and extinguished his own life.

In the journal Sgt. Mack Bolan kept, he wrote: "It looks like I have been fighting the wrong enemy. Why defend a front line 8,000 miles away when the *real* enemy is chewing up everything you love back home? . . ."

So Sgt. Mack Bolan gave himself a discharge from the United States Army and declared his personal war upon the Mafia.

He made no excuses for himself or his totally unlawful acts. Unlawful according to the books. But the books kept the Law from liquidating the Mafia. With their limitless financial resources—illegally gained from extortion, prostitution, gambling, shylocking, take-overs of unions, and drug smuggling and distribution—the Mafia Families diverted billions of dollars into their secret coffers, many of them legitimate fronts. First, because the ruthlessly all-powerful Capone in Chicago got flattened by the income tax guys. Then the man whom all *mafiosi* thought utterly untouchable—the Main Man who had *the fix in*—got busted, Charley Lucky Luciano. Thirty years in the joint. Yeah—he made a deal, which still makes plenty of people wonder, but he got out, only to be deported. That he remained the Main Man until his death no one with any knowledge of the Mafia doubted.

But the survivors learned their lessons fast. Get a front, get nine fronts—a couple restaurants, parking lots, laundries, best of all a junkyard. Anything that does a lot of cash business, with a minimum of paper . . . like canceled checks!

11

Because the Law, tied in knots by the books, rules, restrictions, court decisions, could not get the job done. The Executioner, therefore, dedicated himself to unrestricted warfare. That he fought his *war*, with total commitment, absolute and unwavering belief, made the difference. War is very personal to the fighting man.

It may be logistics, strategy, tactics, or rolls of bumwad to rear-echelon types, but to the man at the point of the spear assaulting the blockhouse, dodging the sizzling hot steel, coming hand-to-hand with the enemy, war has no restrictions if the man expects to survive. The man kills . . . any way he can: stabs, shoots, burns, poisons, ambushes, garrottes, backshoots with a shotgun, or snipes from concealment. That is what war is: to be fought relentlessly and without compromise, and former Sgt. Mack Bolan—The Executioner—was an expert in personal, man-to-man warfare. He would fight his enemy as it had never been fought before.

To that, the Mafia could testify . . . those left alive in Pittsfield, Los Angeles, Frisco, France, London, New York City, Chicago, Vegas—even in their private hideaways on privately owned Caribbean islands. Boston, even the nation's capital, Washington, D.C., San Diego, and utter panic in Philadelphia.

But Mack Bolan had learned something in Philly that scraped his guts hollow.

The Executioner had not been notching his gunstock, keeping score; but he had eliminated well over one thousand mafiosi. He'd believed he'd started thinning them out, only to learn Frankie Angeletti, Don Stefano's faggy "legless" son had imported—smuggled into the U.S.— seventy-five Sicilian *gradigghia:* seventy-five trained, disciplined, badass dudes straight from Sicily; also called *malacarni.* No dictionary defined the word, but Mack Bolan knew what it meant. They were guys who'd shoot

12

your guts full of holes while grinning in your face, and kick your head off as you fell to the ground.

Some old stud *capo* named Don Cafu was supposed to be recruiting, then training these soldiers up to high proficiency and then teaching them some basic English-language skills before shipping them Stateside. Homeplate, Bolan knew, rested somewhere in the Sicilian province Agrigento. The name meant nothing to Mack Bolan. Sicily and the city of Palermo were but dots on a map. It all needed research, he thought hazily.

His first need, though, was medical attention and, even before that, disposal of the sharklike Maserati . . . if he didn't pass out from shock and loss of blood.

1: THE DOCTOR

The doctor Mack Bolan knew never asked questions. His business consisted of tending people able to pay for his professional services. The fees were extremely high, for the doctor edged himself beyond the law every time he admitted a patient to his rooms. His license to practice medicine had long since been lifted. Curiously, he'd been kicked out of the medical profession and convicted of a crime that was no longer a criminal offense in the state of New York, abortion. During the short time he spent in the joint, he'd become acquainted with every type of criminal felon, from baby rapers to safecrackers, hijackers and dope pushers, cheap thieves who popped open soft-drink machines for nickle and dime change, and loft burglars who'd made $200,000 scores hitting a fur vault.

As a former licensed Doctor of Medicine, used to an annual income exceeding $50,000, Wight Byron had no thought whatever upon his release from Sing Sing of acquiring a new trade. Besides, he had customers—Byron called them clients—awaiting: call girls with various professional ailments, friends, or friends of friends he'd made in the penitentary, with gunshot, stab, razor and other wounds, including broken faces and crushed ribs suffered in hit-and-run auto collisions and other incidents of the violent life.

The first thing, of course, upon his release from prison, Byron had to find a source of supply for drugs. Not only dope and painkillers, but antibiotics. Nothing had been easier, because he'd made the proper connections. In fact, he found that he had to distribute his business among half a dozen various pharmacists in order to keep them all happy.

As a front, so the beat cops and precinct sergeants wouldn't get too nosy, Byron opened a secondhand bookshop on the ground floor, with a considerable supply of skinmags, all kinds. This drew crowds. "Clients" in the know had the recognition signals necessary to get past the stud guarding the elevator to the upper rooms, fading from amongst the tit gawkers without notice.

Leo Turrin, the double agent from Pittsfield, had tipped Bolan to Dr. Byron.

Byron stood six feet three, red freckled face, bushy eyebrows, almost colorless gray eyes. He simply nipped the skin along Bolan's ribcage and the slug popped out into his palm. "Ah, yes—"

"Meaning what?" Bolan demanded. "Infected."

"Of course. How long has it been in there?"

"Long enough to become infected. Can you fix it?"

"I would imagine—"

"No, that's not what I asked. Can you fix it? Now."

"I'll have to call for certain medication."

"No phone calls, doc." With singular effort of will, Bolan pushed himself up from the dressing table, rested a moment, head swimming dizzily, swung his legs off and sat resting a moment longer. He gazed hazily around the

16

cubicle, finally focused his eyes on the glass-fronted cabinet with shelves holding bottles. He slid off the table, staggered, caught his balance, lunged across the narrow space and caught his balance again, and once more through sheer effort of will focused his eyes.

He reached up slowly and slid back one of the glass doors. He reached inside and pulled down a bottle holding thick yellowish, creamlike liquid—antibiotics.

Bolan clutched the bottle, fell around with his weight pinning him against the table below the glass case. He held the bottle forward. "Give me a hit, doc. I mean a hit, a massive injection."

"It could kill you."

"It will kill me if I don't. I can smell it now. The wound's gone septic."

Byron nodded.

"You still want to make a phone call, doc?"

"I should."

"Why?"

Wight Byron shrugged, just one tiny fraction too elaborately so Bolan knew. He *knew*. A conscienceless doctor would not hesitate to collect $100,000. And this dude had a setup he could never have unless he'd "mobbed up" while in the joint. Mobbed up meant Mafia, Cosa Nostra, whatever the hell they called it nowadays.

Bolan breathed deeply, and again, and twice more, hyperventilating, pumping his bloodstream full of oxygen. His vision cleared and he felt strength returning to his tired, aching legs. "How you like it, doc?"

Genuinely puzzled, Byron asked, "Like what?"

"Life. Living. Booze and broads and feeling safe, like it'll last forever. You'll never grow old, be bald, need eyeglasses, being a Main Man."

"I don't understand." Once more the just slightly too elaborate shrug.

"Man, listen to me. I don't go naked in the world. You

17

hit me a massive dose of this medication, or I'll blow you up where you stand."

Wight Byron felt the icy blue gaze sink holes through his face, and knew he'd die in his tracks if he failed to oblige this big, broad, scarred deadly man, who should by every logic be dead, wounded as he was. The bastard was shot to pieces. Leg, face, torso. Christ!

Byron moved to the table, carefully. He took up a syringe. He held it before his body in plain sight so the big bastard saw the tube and needle clean. He took the bottle from Bolan's big bony fist, inserted the needle, drew off a massive dosage of the creamlike medication.

Without instructions, Bolan made it to the dressing table and bent over it. He watched Byron over his shoulder. The doc slapped Bolan's butt a stinging smack, and immediately thereafter, when the muscle relaxed, Byron shafted the needle to the hilt and pushed the plunger.

Bolan climbed back up on the table and let the doctor dress his leg wound. He took a smear of stinging Merthiolate, then sulfa salve on the face wound, and a big dressing. That would help conceal his identity, possibly. Something like the clear-lensed, big, dark-framed eyeglasses he sometimes wore, and the moustache and bleached hair.

Bolan lay for a moment resting, and then knew he had to kill the man.

Maybe it was the man's basic character. Possibly those things he'd learned in the joint. Maybe Byron just had consuming greed.

A hundred grand was a hell of a lot of money, tax free.

The man from hell ground felt a drowse come upon him, and he fought with every last bottom gut he had. Someway, somehow, despite Mack Bolan's scrutiny, Dr. Byron had hyped him, the lousy son of a—

Bolan forced himself upright. He swung his legs off the table. On the table below the glass case, four feet

18

from him, he saw an open medical instrument tray. He launched himself with all his superior strength, scrabbled for a scalpel, and just as Byron said, "Hello," into the wall telephone, Mack Bolan plunged the point of the razorlike blade into the base of the man's skull.

Wight dropped dead instantly.

Leaning against the wall, Bolan groped for the telephone, listened a moment, then in the best imitation of Byron's voice he had off the cuff, The Executioner said, "Never mind," and hung up.

Bolan locked the door. Fighting the effects of the unknown drug Byron'd hyped him with, he staggered across the room to the single window. He raised it, looked down into a concrete well littered with trash, thirty feet below. Bolan went back to the dressing table. His efforts and physical movements seemed to overcome the drug's effects. He peeled the sheets off the table, took one and tied it around the table with a square knot. He took the second sheet, tore it into big strips and tied them to the first sheet around the table. He shoved the table to the wall directly under the window, and tossed the loose end of the linen "rope" out of the open window. He flopped, belly-down on the table and slithered out the window, gripped the dangling sheet and began easing himself down. He'd gone ten feet when the cloth in his hands began ripping. In an instant he dropped three feet. Then the fabric held. Gingerly, Bolan went down, hand under hand, and the sheeting ripped again, dropping him another breathless four feet. He hung on, waiting. There was nothing else to do but wait.

The sheet held. Bolan went hand under hand down again, one, two, three—

And then, with the razzling sound of a burpgun's ripping burst, the sheeting ripped apart and dropped him free-fall to the bottom, smashing into the unyielding concrete.

2: SNAKE

As a lad born and raised in a Massachusetts metropolitan area, The Executioner, also known as Mack Bolan, knew virtually nothing of serpents, whether tame or wild, harmless or deadly.

After some twelve years in the army, and two tours in Nam where poisonous snakes killed men in the jungles, and huge tigers carried them off clamped between saber-like teeth, Sgt. Mack Bolan became educated.

Men in his command helped, the kids off Arizona ranches, New Mexico farms, Texas cotton patches.

The way a man's absolutely sure he's killed a snake as it makes an effort to slither silently, unnoticed, with deadly intent into a man's sleeping bag, is by cutting off the head.

Chop it, with a K–Bar knife. Or an entrenching tool. Stomp it, if you have the guts and can move that fast. Use a long-bladed machete.

Or just shoot the son of a bitch.

But you have to get the *head*.

Maybe it was . . . and perhaps it was not . . . some old hill-country or backwoods tale: if you chopped a snake apart but left his head, his brain, alive; he could—and *would*—grow another, new, bigger, better, more powerful length.

Fantasy. Fiction. Truth.

Mack Bolan did not know. He had all he could handle with the problem of personal survival.

When the ripped sheet dropped him free-fall, he'd expected death. But the drug the treasonous doctor had given him affected Mack's depth perception. He fell perhaps ten feet. He was not sure. He sprained slightly the ankle on the same leg where the wound from Philly stung like fire. Otherwise, he got away clean. For five blocks.

It may be true you can never find a cop when you want one, and it may be true, Bolan thought, you always have one belch down your throat when a cop's the last thing on earth you hope to see. But there he stood. The word was *big*.

Mack Bolan stood over six feet by a considerable margin, and weighed more than two hundred pounds, naked and bone dry. The cop scooped Mack Bolan up virtually one-handed, slammed him against the wall of a building near Lexington and East 27th and in a voice that conveyed absolute fearlessness, the cop said, "Okay, asshole, what about it?"

Dredging up from some long ago memory, Mack Bolan said, "I'm diabetic."

The huge cop shoved his hooked nose in Mack's face, sniffed loudly, said, "Okay, you're not drunk," then walked fast to the callbox on the corner. Minutes later Mack lay on the litter in an ambulance en route to Bellevue.

The ambulance crew off-loaded him, rolled the wheeled stretcher into the corridor and left Mack near the door of an emergency treatment room. He got up and walked out the door.

He had to stop and rest three times, but he made it back to the parking lot where he'd left the shark-like Maserati. He expected what he found, after scouting. Two *malacarni* stood patient watch.

He waited almost an hour, resting, building his strength and lasting power before he took the first. He came in low, behind, in sock feet, chopped the hardened ridge of his right half-doubled fist just under the soldier's ear and caught him as he fell backwards, unconscious.

Mack lowered the heavy bulk to the concrete, frisked, came up with a .38 snubnosed, twelve rounds extra ammo, and nine hundred dollars cash in ten and twenty dollar bills. It figured. Soldiers carried misdemeanor bond or bribe dough as a matter of course.

The Executioner put the loose ammo in his right trousers' pocket, stuffed the cash in his left pocket. He stripped the lightweight suitcoat off the soldier, wadded it around the .38 and shot the *malacarni* through the left cheek of his butt . . . all meat, not deadly, a muffled sound.

A moment later, from across the parking lot, Bolan heard the other man call out, softly, "Lou! Hey, you Lou. . . ! That you?"

Bolan grumbled an unintelligible noise.

"Lou—?"

Bolan muttered again.

"Lou, goddammit!"

Bolan heard the shuffle of heavy feet, and a moment later saw the shape of a big man move from the shadows.

"Lou!"

"Here," Bolan called, muffling his mouth with his left hand. "Help—hurt—!"

The big shape broke into a run.

Bolan timed it perfectly.

23

As the big shape came running in, Bolan raised himself to a crouch, planting both heels solidly, and when the man came into range, he swung. His right fist, still holding the snubnosed revolver for grip and solidity, burying into Big Shape's guts, and the man *haaawffed* violently.

Bolan reached and gripped, tangling his left hand in Big Shape's greasy long hair, and jerked the head down as he rose in a single smooth motion and drove his knee upwards into the blurred face.

Bolan's knee met the face and he felt the whole nose go and some upper teeth. He jerked the head up and lowered his knee and smacked them together again, felt the man sag, and as he went down Bolan chopped the snubnose across the back of the man's head.

Once more Bolan had to rest.

He slumped beside the two unconscious forms, himself almost equally out of it. He was human, too. No matter what they said. Whoever in the hell *they* were . . . the assholes, the cops, Leo Bragnola, that Fed in Philly.

Oh God, thought Mack Bolan, I am so tired.

I am shot to pieces and I've been drugged and slammed up against a brick wall and it seems like I've walked halfway across Manhattan. If they came to take me now— *whoever* the hell they are—I couldn't even defend myself.

But I've got to get the snake! The evil, slithering, totally cold-blooded *snake*. Chop off his head. Back in the old country. Homeplate. Don Cafu's ballpark.

Through sheer effort of will, Bolan made himself roll over to his hands and knees and crawl forward. He had Big Shape's gun, his fat wallet, and was going through the rest of the man's pockets when he heard slow, deliberate footsteps approaching along the parking lot's concrete paving.

3: PURLOINED LETTER

Bolan dropped Fat's wallet and rolled over on his butt, bracing his back against the Maserati. It felt like lifting a ton, but he managed to bring the .38 Special snubnosed Detective Special up and gripped it with both hands, aiming into the dark toward the sound of approaching footsteps.

With effort, he cocked the hammer. He wanted to be sure his first shot killed. With the gun cocked, all he had to do was touch the trigger, breathe on it, and *pow!* He was afraid he'd throw the shot wide, pulling all the way through, double-action.

But at the slight, metallic sound of cocking, four distinct clicks, the footsteps halted.

Bolan wearily drew up his legs and braced his locked elbows on his knees, holding the revolver in his right hand with his left cupped around the bottom of his right fist.

A time without end passed.

With activity, Bolan had fought off the effects of the drug, but now in the silent dark, drowsiness washed over him.

He felt his hands sag under the weight of the gun and jerking himself awake, almost loosed a wild shot.

He swore at himself. Combat rule number one—how many kids had he pounded that into out in Nam? Don't reveal your position!

Bolan knew he could not last much longer.

He felt as though he'd lost a quart of blood. And he now bled afresh, feeling the sticky, wet clammy red running down his leg, and the wound in his side had opened again. His eyelids weighed tons. His chin sagged toward his chest.

He fought it, letting go the brace with his left hand, reaching back and cruelly pinching the back of his neck. The stinging pain made him gasp. He opened his mouth wide so the sides stretched as though a dentist had both hands inside his mouth, and Bolan breathed silently, deeply, in and out, oxygenating again. He dropped his left hand and felt around the concrete floor and found Lou's revolver. He picked it up, opened the cylinder, dumped the six bullets into his lap, caught two more bottom-reaching deep breaths, then with a backhand flip, Bolan tossed the gun skittering out across the concrete floor.

The instant he threw the gun, Bolan gripped the other Colt with both hands, waiting for the muzzle flash.

None came.

Bolan waited.

Then he heard a soft, low chuckle.

A moment later Leo Turrin said, "Good move, Sarge . . . but I stopped falling for that one years ago."

"You son of a bitch."

"Easy, Sarge. I'm coming out now. You shoot me and I'll never speak to you again."

"Come on." Bolan let the hammer down on the cocked

26

revolver, holding his left thumb between the shank and the frame, then easing his thumb free when he had a solid hold and knew the hammer would not get loose from him and strike the cap of the bullet hard enough to fire.

"You crazy bastard," Leo said conversationally. "Why'd you leave the hospital?"

"Why would any hunted animal spring a trap?"

"Crazy."

"Sure."

"I mean it. Last place in the world either side would look for you. Like the purloined letter in Poe's story. The fuzz couldn't find it because it lay right before their eyes in plain sight, while they searched all the dark nooks and crannies and looked for secret sliding panels."

"Fiction."

"So?"

Bolan dropped his head, eyes closing. "How'd you find me?"

"A friend of friends spotted you coming into town." Leo kicked the Maserati's front tire. "Whizzing across the bridge in this shark wasn't the smartest move you ever made."

"Going to that doctor *you* set up for me turned out worse."

"Look who's getting choosy."

"The bastard hyped me, even while I watched every move he made."

"A hundred Large is a lot of dough, Sarge."

"Original thought . . . so what's next?"

"Hospital."

"That's crazy. I'd be wide open."

"Okay, you stubborn bastard, have it your way. Hit the streets in Wild Card Johnny's wheels again and look for a pad. Walk around leaking blood. Lie here and pass out—and when the Talaferi send more soldiers to find

27

out what happened to these two assholes, they can carry you home like a baby asleep in momma's arms."

Leo spat on the gleaming hood of the Maserati.

"You're the man, Sarge. You tell me."

"I'm sick. I've got to have help."

"Why the *hell* you think I'm here?" Leo spat again. "For kicks, to watch you play John Wayne?" Leo's voice took on a cruelly mocking tone. "It's okay, men, I'm only shot through the heart, both lungs and the head. Semper Fi and gung-ho, let's climb Surabachi and plant Old Glory."

Leo moved and leaned against the car beside the Maserati. "I hate like hell to muddy the image, Sarge; but this ain't *that* war, and nobody's arranged for a photographer."

"You bastard."

"As a matter of fact, I have papers to prove my father and mother were married for more than two years prior to my birth."

Leo's voice went hard as a keg of nails. "Now how about it? I've got my ass stuck out a mile on both sides of the fence. You want help or not?"

It tore Mack Bolan's heart, but he said, "Help me, Leo."

The nurse was not only young but delightfully pretty. Thick dark hair, high pert bosom, narrow waist, underslung bottom, and legs with good meaty calves the way Mack Bolan liked legs on women, the all-too-rare times he could think about them. High-fashion could cram it. And hospitals could cram all these needles and tubes and most particularly the dripping bottles.

Handcuffs, leg-irons, and chains bolted to concrete walls could not have been more effective, but Bolan could have ripped loose and disengaged himself in seconds.

But the limber rubber tubes, the long needles taped into his arms, the clear glass bottles—they represented Life.

28

And Mack Bolan wanted Life desperately.

Not because he feared death. Long ago he passed that point in time and maturity. He no longer even prayed for himself, feeling he deserved nothing, but only for his brother, Johnny, and Val, and some pals . . . as well as the souls of men rotting in Nam graves who would always be young and fair, for the dead grow no older.

Mack Bolan just did not believe in leaving jobs unfinished. A war not won came under the heading of unfinished business, and had the stink of defeat. No alternative for victory existed, so Mack Bolan's business had not ended.

He had a snake to kill.

Meantime, Mack Bolan's major concern was survival. Deads accomplished nothing, except stinking up the place.

The pert, high-bosomed girl, Mack's day nurse, had tentatively earned his possible trust. The night nurse—no.

She wore a name-plate reading, "M. Minnotte, R.N."

The name did not concern Bolan. Long ago he learned Italian did not equal Mafia. What did concern him was that M. Minnotte had not become his night nurse until a week after he'd been in hospital, and he'd never seen a hand so free with the needle. M. Minnotte would have hit him with a slug of dope every half hour, had Mack wanted it. And when he did not want it, she pouted.

And one other thing. M. Minnotte should never have been a night duty nurse. She had far too much seniority. In a mature way, she also possessed twice the beauty and a dozen times the raw sexuality of pert little dark-haired, "D. Douglass, R.N." Minnotte was the kind any reasonable man would expect to screw her way right up to Head Nurse, competent or not.

Yet, after a week, here she was Mack Bolan's night nurse, and wielding an ever-ready syringe.

Mack knew then . . . the Talaferi had found him.

4: BREAK-OUT

Despite his personal feelings, Leo Turrin was wondering whether Mack Bolan's time had finally come.

Not only had Bolan almost blown Leo Turrin's cover more than once, but The Executioner seemed to be getting much too careless with his own life.

Leo Turrin was a double.

He had been born into and held a *capo,* "boss" ranking in his hometown Mafia. His specific job was Chief Whoremonger. Leo himself "turned out" Mack Bolan's sister, Cindy . . . made a call girl prostitute of her.

At the same time, Leo Turrin, former Green Beret, was a federal agent, and in that direction lay his true allegiance.

For that reason, reinforced by Leo's admiring, hard-won affection, he had not killed Mack Bolan in the parking lot. It was not the first time Leo'd had the time, place, and opportunity.

All the same, Bolan had become a pain in the ass. Everytime Leo helped Bolan, he jeopardized his own security. Not that Leo spent so much time "taking care" of the guy. Bolan possessed every instinct of a jungle cat; he was all bone and gristle with a remorseless desire for survival no matter who or what he killed to keep himself alive. So far he was succeeding beyond anyone's wildest dreams—or nightmares.

And yet, at the same time, Leo knew, Bolan was a gentle man, compassionate, loving and tender toward his younger brother. And then there was the girl, Val. . . .

But playing both sides of the street could get Leo Turrin killed and he knew it. Dead, he would be totally without value to his government; and he honestly, truly believed that as an insider, a Mafia *capo,* he served better, performed his duties more responsibly, and had a hell of a lot longer to live than he did bodyguarding Mack Bolan.

Goddammit, he told himself, I did all I could. I got him into the hospital. I checked out *everyone* who might come near him, doctors, nurses, LVNs, even the scrubwomen and male hall orderlies.

Yet, something kept nagging at the back of Leo's mind. He cursed himself for having been a Special Forces officer, and having spent too much time with the CIA on special assignment. Having infiltrated VC and NVR lines, penetrated the enemy's innermost secrets any way he could—women, dope, liquor, catering to bestial tastes and human perversions.

Afterwards, Leo wondered *why?*

Why he'd said, "Yes," and meant it, when a certain highly placed government official asked him to become a double after serving with the Special Forces in Southeast Asia.

In the beginning, Leo's reasons had been simple. He loved his country. He'd fought for it and learned to love it all the more, because during the fighting he'd learned

32

how excessively inhuman the alternative of communism was, and upon his return to civilian life he found great similarities between communistic and Mafia philosophies—namely, the end justified any and all means, treachery, terrorism, death, tyrannical rule. The best example Turrin could remember had occurred when he was only a child.

An innocuous little man named Arnold Schuster spotted the notorious bank robber Willie Sutton and notified the police. Sutton was arrested, and even though he had no connection whatever with the Mafia, a ferociously bloodthirsty Mafia underboss named Albert Anastasia ordered one of his soldiers, Fredrick Tenuto, to kill Schuster. This would serve as an object lesson to all would-be "squealers"—Mafia or ordinary good citizens. Then to cover himself, Anastasia had Tenuto murdered, and so well disposed of that twenty years later Tenuto's body has never yet been found.

Also, Leo Turrin had enjoyed some degree of formal education, so his decision to become a "double" had an intellectual basis, as well as moral and patriotic. So it was that Leo found himself helping Bolan out when he called, knowing the consequences if he was caught.

Turrin delivered Bolan's "tools." Then he got the hell out. He had no desire to witness what was about to happen, and his absences from Pittsfield had become increasingly harder to explain, the Mafia being a subculture constantly beset by undercurrents of intrigue, deceit, and murderous treachery. If Leo didn't stay home and take care of his business, one of his underbosses would start getting the idea he no longer needed Leo, and Leo would find himself wearing concrete coveralls at the bottom of Onota Lake west of the city.

"Okay," Turrin said, dropping the heavy canvas duffle bag on the foot of the bed. "Everything's here, info about

33

the homeland, plus a bonus. I turned the Maserati over for fifteen grand, minus my commission."

"Commission!"

"Goddam right. I don't contribute my professional services free of charge. Besides that, I have to keep my head right, my thinking, you dig, Sarge? I stop thinking like a *capo,* first thing I'm not acting like a *capo,* and my ass is stuck out a mile. That, my friend, I don't owe you." Leo grinned like a wolf. "It wasn't all that easy, either. The Talaferi Family had a notion it should inherit their hitman's Maserati when you brought Cavaretta down."

"Okay, you earned it."

"And I'm taking it." Leo patted his hip where his wallet rested. "I won't ask your plans, because you would lie or not answer at all. Just do me one favor. Make your next blitz as far from me as you can get."

"That's a promise."

"You're kidding."

"I never joke about what I'm doing."

Leo stared at Bolan, curious and puzzled, but he knew better than to ask any questions. While Bolan dressed in his black combat garb and armed himself with the silencer-equipped Beretta and the silver .44 Automag, four frag grenades and extra ammo clips for both guns, Leo kept watch at the door, and told Bolan:

"I only saw four, but there were two cars, both with wheelmen, set at the northeast and southwest corners. I figure at least six and maybe more." Matter-of-factly, Leo added, "You know the nurse is in on it?"

"I figured it out."

"She's a hype, among other things."

"I'll get the pedigree later. You better haul ass . . . and thanks."

Warmly, Leo said, *"Arrivederci,"* and stepped out into the hall closing the door behind him, leaving the room in darkness.

Bolan waited. He found the waiting neither hard nor easy, but a neutral something he had long, long ago learned to endure. Waiting was as much a part of warfare as trying to stay alive. Waiting for chow, for mail, for relief, to leave for some new place or arrive after a long journey. Except that now, for Mack Bolan, the man in black, The Executioner, waiting had become an occupation with singular purpose; he was waiting for the enemy to show himself.

The room was in almost total darkness, door closed, shades drawn. A sliver of light came from under the bathroom door, just enough to back-light them when they came. Bolan had figured the geometry of the room and then positioned himself.

The woman came first.

Bolan expected that. They would want him alive. They wanted no more mistakes, no more wrong heads delivered to collect the bounty.

Minnotte entered soundlessly and crossed to the bed with stealth a cat could envy. She stopped, and Bolan knew she was letting her eyes grow accustomed to the dark. After a long minute, she reached forward with her left hand and peeled the covers back as she leaned toward the bed, syringe ready in her right hand.

Bolan took her then.

He clamped one big hand over her mouth and nose and at the same time plucked the syringe from her hand. He held her fast with all his strength, immobilizing her except for the soft scuffing of her rubber-soled white shoes. He brought the syringe up, and sticking the needle in the side of her neck, pushed the plunger.

Bolan had no idea what he'd hyped her with, but the virtually instantaneous effect of the drug frightened him. In seconds the nurse became a slack, unconscious weight and he let her fall forward on the bed, picked up her feet and rolled her over on her back, laid out straight. Quickly, he wiped the syringe with a sheet and put it into Minnotte's right hand. Then he stepped back into the shadows, waiting again. He drew the Beretta, eased back the slide and checked with his finger that the gun had a round chambered and ready to fire. He checked the safety: off.

Two men came next, throwing open the door and rolling in a wheeled stretcher, quickly closing the door behind them, snapping on the light. "Okay, Minnie. What the—"

The soldier reached under his phony white hospital orderly coat and Bolan shot him between the eyes. He dived across the bed as the other man ducked low and pulled the stretcher over as a shield. Bolan pulled off three shots, spacing them along the length of the stretcher's underside. Both the second and third *phutts* from the silenced pistol brought screams of pain.

That meant two down of a probable six, and maybe more.

And Mack Bolan was trapped inside a hospital room five stories above ground. No going out the window here on sheets tied together, especially if the soldiers had been stationed properly. He'd be a target so easy, pasted against the wall, the soldiers would have time to send home for their wives to come share the victory.

Bolan jumped back over the bed, jerked the stretcher aside, fell to his knees as the wounded soldier snapped off a shot Bolan felt clip through his hair. The blast resounded like a cannon shot in the small room, even loosening plaster and raising dust.

Bolan shot the man through the bridge of the nose.

He righted the stretcher, opened the door, heaved the first dead onto the punctured sheets, face down, then shoved the stretcher out into the hallway.

They had both ways covered. Shots came from the right and the left, almost simultaneously. Bolan reached back

36

and got the second dead, dragged him to the door, heaved him upright, then shoved him out.

As the body toppled out into the hallway, shots came again.

Bolan followed, squirming flat on his belly, as the shots at the dead man went high. He turned left, sighted and gutshot the soldier who stood like an old-time gunfighter, legs spread wide, arm thrust full-length, sighting. The man doubled in the middle, screaming, fell backwards, dropping his gun and holding his guts.

Bolan rolled over twice, taking what cover the two dead men and the toppled stretcher afforded. A shot knocked a jagged hole in the tile floor four inches from Bolan's elbow. All along the hallway, patients screamed in terror. A nurse came rushing out of one room between Bolan and the live gunman, and the soldier used her as a shield to pop up and snap off a shot. The woman fell and Bolan thought she'd been hit, but she'd only fainted because he heard the *crack* overhead, then the bullet whacking into the wall.

Mack Bolan had never killed an innocent person, never harmed one, nor any cop. He had, in fact, allowed himself to be shot by Leo Turrin's wife rather than kill her when she began pumping slugs at him from fifteen feet with a tiny .25 automatic back when The Executioner first declared war on the Mafia.

But now. . . .

Maybe it had come to that point.

If he tried to turn and run down the hallway toward the open end—where the gutshot soldier moaned continuously in pain—he left his back open for the other gunman. The hallway was too narrow for jinking, zig-zagging with any real hope for success.

With regret, Mack Bolan snapped off the last shots in the Beretta magazine to keep the gunman's head down, and at the same time unclipped one of his grenades,

37

pulled the pin, let the spoon fly, and with a swift, hard underhand snap-toss, skittered the frag down the hallway.

He punched the button on the pistol, dropped the empty clip, pulled a full one from the leg pocket of his black combat suit and shoved it home, racked back the slide and chambered a round. He drew himself up into a coiled muscular readiness, and when the frag went in a thunderous roar of noise, dust, and whizzing shrapnel, Bolan charged.

He was almost sick with relief when he reached the end of the hallway and found the grenade had gone off in to the stairwell and exploded between floors, and the only person hurt was the Mafia soldier who lay dead, his back shredded.

Bolan went down the stairs at a full run. His only chance lay in total and complete surprise.

He got past the fourth, then the third floor without interference, except for hospital personnel who kept trying to "capture" him, while screeching questions.

As he broke loose and dropped free-fall five steps, then to the landing between the third and second floors, he came face to face with two gunmen. He hesitated only a fraction of a second, saw neither man wearing a police shield, then Bolan pumped two shots into each man, one, one, then one and one again, insurance.

That was six, at least two more, the wheelmen, and somewhere down here Bolan knew the crew leader waited. Standard Operating Procedure, S.O.P., for Mafia hits, contracts. The crew leader never does the work himself except as a last resort. He uses young punks on the make, kids looking for a "sponsorship" into a Family, proving their worthiness by doing the dirty work. Sometimes they got paid off in lead, or concrete blankets, like Tenuto when he hit Schuster on Anastasia's orders.

Noise no longer mattered, so as he charged out onto the ground floor, Mack holstered the Beretta and drew the huge silver .44 Automag. A security guard with drawn revolver stopped, mouth agape, started to bring his gun into action and Mack shot a hole in the floor three feet to the side of the guard's right foot. The thundering explosive power of the .44's muzzle blast and the shattered tile stinging his legs proved too much for the guard. He broke sideways, ducking low, and ran for cover.

Mack went through the front door with such speed and power the doorframe sprung loose from its hinges. And then he was outside, in the dark, in the open where he could use his experience and cunning.

Bolan saw the cars. They had been positioned well. One at each opposite corner, so the wheelmen could see a side and front, or the other side and back of the hospital. Just as Leo said. Bolan stopped in the dark shadows cast by the tall building, rested his shoulder against the brick, blew off one wheelman's head as the man opened the door and got out, gun in hand.

Bolan ran for the car. As he crossed the street, the other car came rocketing around the corner, closing on him. Bolan dropped to his left knee, brought the Automag up and held it in both hands, and pumped three shots through the oncoming grillwork. The engine exploded and the car swerved, hit the curb, toppled over on its side, then rolled slowly over on its top.

Bolan dragged the dead wheelman from the car at his side, got in and drove away.

An hour later, Bolan stepped through the back door of a Village shop, attracted the attention of an elderly clerk, and a half-hour later emerged with a wardrobe somewhat more "fashionable" than suited his personal tastes; but he'd chosen the shop because the clerks were accustomed to freaks in such far-out clothing the gray-haired lady hardly looked at Bolan's black combat garb while outfitting him. Twenty minutes later, Bolan rented a shabby furnished room, slept until dawn, then hit the street again in his new clothes and found another shop which sold clothing of more conservative and nondescript styles. Here, Bolan completely outfitted himself, underwear outwards, for the long trip. Then he went to see a man about some papers.

5: FLIGHT

Captain Charles Teaf felt like an ass. Ten minutes ago he'd been inside the company office wishing like hell he could get a good charter, maybe to Cleveland or Chi. But it was probably raining both those places, too. Miami or Phoenix were too much to hope for, on this soggy wet day at Teterboro Airport, New Jersey. He had might as well wish for the friggin' moon, or another trip to Rome like he'd had ten days ago.

That was ten minutes ago. He'd been grousing around the office, and hinting to Annabelle maybe they could slip back to the long-range jet, the one with seats on the starboard side aft that made down into a bunk, and rip off a little. But the gloomy day must have been working on her, too. She told him to go commit an impossible act with himself. As though she had some kind of treasure, saving it for the right guy.

What a laugh. Forty, if she was a day, but she sometimes worked stew on charter jobs. The thing was, hardly anyone ever noticed her face. With tits like she had who cared? Throw a flag over the face and go for Old Glory. Just what the hell else she did, Captain Charles Teaf was not quite sure. A little typing, answered the phone, spent a hell of a lot of time examining freight manifests, and when not in the office she was out walking the line, talking to guys and gals from the competition.

That was ten minutes ago, when Teaf's mind was occupied with speculation upon whether Annabelle wore a 44D- or 42DD-cup bra. Now he had something important on his mind. Around aviation's somewhat incestuous circles, Captain Charles Teaf had an acknowledged reputation. The word was *greedy*. He would backshoot his nice little old gray-haired mother for a guaranteed profit.

But Teaf found the man with the money rather frightening. A big, icy-eyed bastard with a bandage on his face who walked with a slight limp. And who insisted on such privacy that Captain Teaf stood outside in the goddam rain talking to him. Teaf's stiffly starched white shirt had turned to clammy glue against his skin, his fancy black shoulder boards with wide gold stripes dripped, and he knew the large wings above his left shirt pocket would need cleaning and polishing because they were brass, not gold.

The thing was, the big bastard with the chilly eyes had a big fist full of money. But the guy had not let go of any of it yet. Teaf could hardly keep his eyes off the green. He knew it had to be some kind of smuggling job. That did not bother Teaf at all. He'd been *there* before. Except dope. Dope was too heavy. Dope was IN now, The Big Thing, with the feds, state and city and county cops, DAs; dope was Big, on TV, in the papers, so to hell with dope.

Some creep might cave in his wife's skull for cheating on him and he'd hit the bricks an hour later on $1500 bond. Some college punk with a half-kilo of grass went so

42

far back in the slammer they had to pipe air to him, $25,000 bond. So no dope, no matter how much money the big bastard offered.

Christ, the big son of a bitch looked like he could snap a man in half with his bare hands, and he had a presence —brutal, as though he had cracked a few spines, crushed some ribs, snapped a neck or two.

"Cut the crapping around and answer me," Bolan said. "What's the charter rate, long-range jet, to Italy?"

The company would hang Teaf if he lied. "I can't kid you, mister. Or lie to you. Against company rules. Commercial carrier is cheaper."

"If I wanted that, Teaf, I wouldn't be here."

The big bastard fanned out the wad. If he had a dime he held twenty grand in those big hands. And how the hell does he come to know my name?

"Okay, mister, I've told you. The airlines are cheaper. You dig?"

"I dig. Talk to me."

"I don't know what you want yet, so I can't quote a price firm."

"Look, ace, I didn't come here to stand in the rain and bullshit. *You* dig?"

Before Teaf could answer Bolan said, "I want a private, long-range jet charter to Naples. For starters. There may be more work. I can give you a ten grand deposit. *Will* that get you moving?"

"Just one thing, mister. No dope. Absolutely nothing involving dope."

"I ought to break your face."

"Okay, okay, get hot, but just so you understand."

"The ten Large do it?"

"Well, depends on the party, baggage, freight if any, crew, maybe a particular *kind* of stew you want—" Teaf leered.

"Get cute one more time, ace, and watch me vanish.

This airport's full of grounded airplanes and non-flying pilots."

"Deal!" Captain Teaf said fast.

"Okay, I'm the only passenger. I have one crate of cargo and some personal baggage. No other crew. You alone."

"When do you wish to leave, sir?"

"I don't want the crate opened by Italian customs. That's why I came to you. It's not dope. You know that. Nobody carries crap from the outhouse to the bedroom, right?"

"Can it sting me?"

"Heavy, cap. That's what the bonus is for."

"I've seen no bonus."

Bolan peeled ten hundred-dollar bills from the wad and stuck them between the bottom two buttons of Teaf's shirt. He peeled another Large out and let Teaf have a look at it, then stuffed that inside the captain's shirt.

"There's another three G after we get the crate past customs."

Teaf nodded. "Like I said, deal." Teaf placed his hand on his belly and rubbed, feeling the green against his skin under his wilted shirt.

"When do you want to depart, sir?"

"Now."

"You mean *right* now?"

"Exactly."

"No way, man."

"Hand the bread back, ace."

Teaf backed away. "Wait! I mean you need a passport, visa, innoculation certificates, all that stuff."

"I've got them."

"You . . . have?"

"My baggage and freight's ready to load."

"Well, Jeez. I can't believe this. I mean only ten days ago I lucked out . . . I mean a trip to Rome, some rush job for an oil company—"

"So, what are you saying?"

"Hell, man, I'm ready, too. I got *all* the papers. For myself *and* the aircraft. I mean, Jeez, it's like some kind of miracle, you know?"

"Not exactly," Mack Bolan said. "I shopped around."

It was the only way to go.

As Mack Bolan had told the treacherous doctor: The Executioner did not go naked in the world, unarmed. Doing so invited certain death. The Mafia, the Outfit, the Organization, Cosa Nostra, whatever the media called it this week or today, still had a $100,000 bounty on Mack Bolan's head. Since he not only double, or was it triple-crossed them, sending their Wild Card's head back to them in a sack, maybe the ante had gone up.

You get what you pay for.

Pay cheap, get cheap.

Blank check, expect the best. And have the right to demand it, by god!

The Executioner *knew* the bounty had gone up. The sum he did not know, only that the Outfit would never stand for what he'd done, panic in Philly. Once more, he'd rigged it so the Families became involved in unremitting warfare against each other. The last thing in the universe they wanted.

What am I worth to them now? Bolan wondered.

A quarter mill?

A half?

The whole wad?

One million dollars?

Why not? Even the most conservative "experts" claim organized crime milks the U.S. public of $40 *billion* a year. A billion is a thousand million.

"I can't think," Bolan wrote in his journal, "of figures that size. They are an endless number of zeroes to me, unreal, meaningless, and yet *actual*. Nickles, dimes, quarters, dollars, entire paychecks, into hock, into shy-locking, vigorish, trapped, becoming prostitutes, numbers runners, pimps, drug pushers."

Bolan had been there.

He had a dead father, and mother, and sister, and maimed brother to show for it. And a girl he loved that he dared not go near, for fear he might be followed.

Once already the bastards had kidnapped his brother Johnny, and Valentina. To get them back alive, he blitzed Boston—a real old-fashioned *lightning war,* and eventual-ly exposed a man in the highest possible influential cir-cles, social and governmental, as just one more asshole.

That's what the cops called criminals. Assholes.

Mack Bolan could think of no better or more descrip-tive word, when he really thought about what happened around that particular area of the human anatomy.

Of course, Bolan had expected his documents source to betray him, after his experience with Dr. Wight Byron.

Strangely, that had gone off with remarkable smooth-ness. Bolan wondered if it had been too smoothly. Think-ing back, he wondered if he'd covered himself well enough, asking not only for the impeccably forged pass-port, but visas to France, Switzerland, and Algeria.

Despite the dollar devaluation, most countries in Eu-rope still eagerly sought the good old U.S. greenback and American tourism, and therefore required no visa what-ever: Ireland, England, West Germany, Spain, Holland and Denmark.

They made it hell for a phony to prove up his *bona fides.*

Maybe the smoothness of his documentation had gone so well because the gut-hollowing footsteps in the parking lot had been those of Leo Turrin. And Mack Bolan knew that backing Leo stood rock-solid Bragnola, and, possibly, Persicone.

46

Bolan could not bring himself to trust most FBI agents, despite the individual behavior of Persicone when panic went through Philly like sand through a tin horn. FBI types were too ambitious. And Mack knew they'd turn on their own kind—other agents, local cops, deputies, state policemen—and nail their hides to the barn wall for "civil rights violations."

Given a million years, Mack Bolan could think of no man who violated more "civil rights" than he did himself in his declared war against organized crime. He was arresting officer, booking desk officer, judge, jury, and Executioner.

About the only thing he did not do, in the Bureau's Book, was whip niggers over the head with pickhandles like guards in some prisons did. Mack never used that word.

The charter flight was the only way Mack Bolan could have gone.

His crate would never have passed U.S. Customs export control. Nor would it have passed the regular, scheduled airline customs in Italy.

But more important than that, Mack had carefully checked out the new antihijacking security procedures at La Guardia and JFK. He saw no possible way he to bypass them while carrying his silencer-equipped Beretta and .44 Automag; and he was not about to enter Don Cafu's ballpark unprepared.

If he played it tight, cool, smart, and had plenty of luck to back him, Bolan knew he'd get one good swing at the first pitch.

And that son of a bitch would be a low outside curve, sure as God made little green apples!

He settled back into the deep cushions of the chartered private jet and tried to get some rest. It would be a long flight.

6: ANNABELLE

Annabelle Caine had worked with and for the Mafia since she was fifteen years old. For the first two years she had not been aware who her employer was. Having excessively matured quite early, she won a beauty contest in her Ohio hometown. That same night the grinning master of ceremonies placed a rhinestone "crown" upon her blonde head, Annabelle learned the price of success. The emcee introduced her to a terribly handsome, mature, swarthy, impeccably tailored individual named Vito Rapace, head judge of the contest. Vito asked permission of Annabelle's widowed star-struck mother to take the lovely young winner out on the town, show her off. He hinted broadly about Hollywood connections. Annabelle would have gone no matter what her mother said. It was simply convenient and time-saving that mother said, *"Yes, Mr. Rapace!"*

Annabelle was not even aware she truly had no beauty,

even skin-deep. She simply had a marvelous set of jugs and Vito Rapace wanted to get his hands on them. That night he did, and took the rest from her, too. After that, Vito became her "sponsor"; she dropped out of school and moved into a Toledo apartment Vito just happened to have vacant at the time. He paid her tuition to a "charm" school and the training gave her a certain superficial gloss—she learned to walk well. Vito dropped by the apartment on the average of three times a week, occasionally bringing another couple, usually Johnny, The Plumber Augurio, and some girl. The girls all looked like they could have been sisters and, Annabelle realized after awhile, a lot like herself. Within six months, after Vito tired of her and she had been passed on to Johnny, then Tonio, and Joe The Sapper, she was a "business girl" and knew it. After once attempting to leave and surviving the consequent beating, she accepted it. After a fashion, she actually did have a career in "pictures." Stills, which were taken by hidden cameras and highly compromised the other "actor"—a cop, or judge, or banker, or president of a labor union.

But Annabelle Caine had an almost feral instinct for personal survival, and she courted favor with her Vito until he let her out of the "business" and worked her into other operations. For awhile she handled the books in a numbers back office, then worked a phone drop, a telephone relay system. She was a sort of middlegirl, who took bets from runners, then phoned them to the bookie's back office. Even if arrested herself, as she twice was, she could tell the cops nothing but a phone number. The bulls didn't even get that much from Annabelle Caine, and Vito knew about it. He moved her up another notch, into a loansharking operation. Then Annabelle created a job for herself.

One evening she drove Vito to the airport. She got a

porter to take care of Vito's baggage, and they went into the bar for a drink until the plane for Newark arrived. She saw her boss off, and this being an early evening flight, Annabelle saw that more than half those who deplaned headed directly for the lounge and a drink. She walked around to the baggage pickup and found it deserted. She watched for an hour. She went back five nights in a row and watched. The sixth night she dressed in large loose coveralls, tucked her hair up into a railroader's cap, wore gloves, borrowed a pickup truck, and twenty minutes after the plane landed, she cleaned out the baggage ramp. She did so again, the next night. The third night she went back, but this time in Vito's car and wearing a tight sweater. She had long since learned that men, and most women, could not identify her face after they had seen her in a tight sweater.

She spotted the plant five minutes after she began walking along the pickup, checking the tags. Two plainclothes bulls in a car parked in the shadows. She put on an act for them. Sure enough, one of the bulls got out of the car and came over, flashed the tin, asked what she was doing.

"I lost all my baggage on a flight three nights ago. I thought maybe it had come in by now."

"Well, I'll tell you, miss," the cop said, "I think maybe you can kiss the stuff goodbye. It was probably stolen."

Annabelle wailed, burst out crying, ran away, leaving the cop with egg on his face. After that she never made more than one hit a month when she wiped the pickup clean. On odd nights and days, she would drive up in different cars, and with a now-practiced-eye, pluck one large expensive bag or one set of luggage, stow it and drive away.

The first six months after she began her own little thing, she had fifty cameras of various values, what

51

eventually turned out to be almost $10,000 worth of jewelry, and several thousand dollars worth of clothing and good quality luggage, even at dime-on-the-dollar selling to a fence.

Then she let Vito in on the scam, it having occurred to her that if the baggage was left unattended much of the air freight probably was also left sitting until shipped or picked up. She staked out the freight ramp and discovered she was right. Vito took it over then, and cut her a big slice plus a terrific bonus for getting on the scam. He was so pleased he started coming around again for a while, then tired of her again. When that happened, Annabelle felt herself in a position to ask a favor. She asked permission to leave town, and Vito agreed, seeing those dollar signs, all her share becoming his.

With the connections Vito gave her, Annabelle moved on to Cleveland, then Chicago, La Guardia, Idlewild, becoming a sort of "traveling instructor and advisor"; but it had gotten too hot, much too heavy by the time Idlewild became JFK, because virtually every theft was an FBI case, an interstate shipment case. It was time to fade, so Annabelle drew in her chest and after a six months vacation at Nassau, she went to work at Teterboro, still the best damn spotter in the business.

But she was getting dull-edged, and smart enough to know it. Plus one other thing. Since she no longer stole anything herself, she needed accomplices. And that's how your ass lands in jail, taking in other people, because you never know how strong they really are until the heat hits. And now that the feds and most states had the immunity law for cop-outs, she was scared and seldom turned anything but cinches, stuff she already had a buyer for, and she cut out the middle guy, letting the "buyer" pick it up himself. It lowered her take, but it also lowered her risks.

Now, on this particular gloomy, wet, gray, filthy day, she felt as out of sorts as everyone else. In fact, she thought, maybe it would be a hell of a good thing if she *did* whip a little on Teaf. She could use a good lay herself, maybe cheer her up. If the son of a bitch just didn't strut so! Like some 25,000-hour senior airline captain, when she knew for a fact Teaf was a TWA reject.

And then the whole world turned rosy for Annabelle Caine.

Mack The Bastard Bolan walked into the office. Just like that. God, ballsy guy, like a goddam cape buffalo! The word was already out, she'd heard it the night before from a contact she still maintained with the organization. Bolan had shot his way out of a trap at the hospital, then vanished.

Except, there he stood! Bolan. The man with $100,000 on his head! Her hands shook as she dialed. But her connection was out of pocket. Oh, the bastard, why couldn't he be shacked up with some—

Christ, they were already rolling out the long-range jet!

Answer the phone, you son of a bitch! I've got a hundred thousand fuckin' dollars standing fifty feet from me! Teaf came in and wrote up the charter, gave Annabelle ten thousand in cash, advised her to call an armored car service immediately because it was risky having that kind of dough.

She could hardly breathe. She dropped the money. Scrabbled around on the floor gathering the bills up. She heard Teaf go out. She couldn't stand it. There he went, getting aboard, a *hundred thousand dollars*. Oh, God, no!

She jerked open the back door and screamed at one of the lineboys. He came running. She thrust the money into his hands and pointed, "Clean it up, call an armored car service, ten thousand," and shoved past him, running,

53

almost tripping in high-heels. She stopped and jerked her shoes off and ran.

Mack Bolan became aware of another presence aboard the aircraft when he felt a slight change in the cabin air pressure. He did not move until he felt the pressure normalize, and heard a faint *click!*

Still lying back in his seat as though asleep, he eased his hand under his jacket and gripped the Beretta, then like a cat, he rolled out of the seat and flat on the floor, pistol aimed.

The girl shrieked: "No!" and shoved her hands out palms forward as though they would stop 9mm Parabellum sizzlers.

Bolan relaxed pressure on the trigger and got to his feet.

Teeth chattering, eyes sprung wide as saucers, the woman managed, "Mr. Borzi . . . can I, can I bring you anything?"

Bolan sat down, motioning her forward. She stopped directly beside the seat. Never in his life had Mack Bolan seen such bosoms. Looking up he could not see her face, only the underside of a brown knit jersey jutting out. Then she leaned over and Mack saw an ordinary face, a few years on it, thin lips, muddy eyes, bad complexion not hidden by pancake. The only thing she had going for her was the tits and she knew it.

Her right hand dropped to Mack's left thigh. "Or anything I can *do* for you?"

"No, darlin,' I'm fine." Mack gestured toward a seat across the narrow aisle. "Sit down."

He noticed she wore a pants suit. Probably had legs as bad as her face, tits the whole show.

"When did you come aboard?"

"While they loaded your crate. *Machinery,* I believe it was stenciled."

54

Mack Bolan did not know for sure, quite yet, positively, but he believed he'd have to kill this girl. Her nose was much too long. He answered. "That's right. Machinery."

"What business are you in?"

"Well, ah, various. Actually, salvage and demolition are my main specialties."

"Of what?"

Mack knew then. He would have to kill her. She played it too clever. Possibly . . . hell, *probably* she had already been down into the cargo hold with a prybar.

"Is there any booze aboard?" Mack asked, as though the thought had just occurred to him.

"Anything you wish," the girl said, smiling. She had good teeth. "Not limited to drinks, I might add."

"So nice to know. If the mood strikes me, dear. What's your name?"

"Annabelle."

"Annabelle, who, what?"

"Just Annabelle."

"Okay, Annabelle no last name, I'll take a Bloody Mary and go very light on the hot."

"Right on, Mr. Bo—oh—orzi."

Well, The Executioner thought, that's a death warrant. My passport and visas and documents and the few travelers' checks he'd bought, all in the name Mike Borzi; but she damned near called me Bolan. And it took her too long to build the drink.

Bolan winked, faked a sip, reached up and touched, found a hard unyielding silicone stiffness and dropped his hand. She had dropped to her knees beside him, hand going to his belt the moment Mack touched her. He acted as though he understood nothing, unlatched his lap strap and rose to his feet and shoved past her.

In the cockpit Teaf lazed back in his seat, the aircraft on flight director, a highly sophisticated autopilot. Bolan shot a look at the altimeter. It showed FL 23: Flight Level 23,000 feet. He glanced past the pilot and looked out the window.

Bolan was not a pilot, though he had flown many hours in Nam and in the Army, in fixed wing aircraft and helicopters. He also had phenomenal eyesight and depth perception. He was not sure they were actually 23,000 feet above the ocean, but knew the airplane was tremendously high.

Laconically, Bolan said, "Christ, we're so high it looks like a calm lake down there."

Teaf roused himself, reached forward, rapped the altimeter sharply, and the big marker moved some forty feet higher. Teaf then twisted the knob on the instrument and set the tiny window marker on the left side of the altimeter to read 29.92 inches mercury, the standard setting for over-ocean flights so all aircraft had the same altimeter reading and would, theoretically, if conforming to assigned altitudes, avoid mid-air collisions.

"We're a little high," Teaf said, but did nothing. The extra forty feet did not seem to bother him.

"What about oxygen?" Mack Bolan/Borzi asked.

"Plane's pressurized, sir. No sweat."

"What if something busts open?"

Condescendingly, expert explaining to frightened novice, Teaf said, "Still no sweat. Get a might cold before we got down to lower altitude, but we have portable ox-bottles all over the ship. The green ones, stashed in niches, with a mask. Notice them?"

"Yeah, but what the hell, man. Like it *goes*, I mean all of a sudden?"

"You mean explosive decompression?" Teaf turned in his seat and grinned at Mack. "No sweat. If you can't reach an ox-bottle soon enough, you might hypoxia, oxygen starvation, and pass out."

Teaf pointed vaguely at the instrument. "But that would show up here instantly and I'd put her down on the deck. Like I said, Mr. Borzi, no sweat."

"Unless I happened to be standing next to a door or window that went, huh?"

With obvious and decided discomfort, Teaf sat up straight in his seat. He did not answer. He took the bizjet off flight director and began flying manually.

Bolan/Borzi jerked up the armrest of the right side pilot seat and sat down sideways so he could look directly at Teaf. Deliberately, he thumbed the pilot in the ribs.

"I don't remember an answer, ace."

Evidently knowing that both silence and lies had become worthless, Teaf shrugged, sighed, and said, "Okay, sure, at this altitude we are pressurized for eight thousand feet while flying at twenty-three thousand. If we had an explosive decompression—extremely unlikely, mind you! —then anything close to the leak would go."

"You mean *ME?*" Bolan/Borzi shouted.

"Oh, no, sir, unless a big, I mean *big hole*. Like a window or door. The chances of that are so remote, hell, I'd give you million to one odds."

"That's a bet," Bolan said, getting to his feet.

"What?"

Bolan did not answer. He returned to the cabin from the cockpit, and as he expected four of the aft seats had been lowered so they made a wide but not too long bed. Immaculately clean, smooth, pale blue silk sheets had been laid across the lowered bed-made seats. Annabelle lay naked on the pale blue.

Bitterly, The Executioner smiled.

He stood at the forward end of the cabin, just outside the cockpit, and called to Annabelle, "Stand up so I can see you. Don't hide such beauty!"

She rose to her knees, incredible bosoms pointed like twin gunmounts straight at Bolan. "I can't stand up. The overhead's too low."

"That's fine. That's beautiful."

She smiled with a brittle, professional brilliance.

"What did you put in my drink, darlin'?" Mack said, "something to kill me, or only knockout drops?"

"*What?*"

"No, darlin', that's *my* question. What?"

For a moment Annabelle stood there on her knees, totally defiant. Without a word uttered she told Mack Bolan:

"I am one of them. I obey the rule. Total silence."

Bolan whipped the pistol from under his left arm, aimed past Annabelle, fired three shots so fast the sounds came as a single blend of noise.

The window behind her naked body vanished, explosively.

Bolan dived sideways to his right, landing on his knees, wrapping his strong long arms around the back of the seat, feeling the decompression whistle past him, carrying with it papers, dust, noise, seat cushions, pillows, seat covers, a candy wrapper, smoke and ashes and cigarette butts, and sucking Annabelle directly into the small window.

Bolan heard her screams.

Maybe if she had been standing upright instead of on her knees it would have made a difference.

As it was, the window lay directly behind her and she went out head first, screeching, stuck for a fraction of an instant, then the window sucked her through—the vast bosom and wide back, then her wide hips slowing movement for another fraction, and then she was gone. The silken blue sheets had vanished. Her clothing, underwear, stockings, shoes.

She might never have existed, ever.

Bolan clamped an emergency oxygen bottle on his face

58

and walked into the cockpit, slipping the pistol out of sight. He sat down in the right seat and held out his open palm.

Teaf pulled his ox-mask from his face long enough to shout, "What the hell, Borzi?"

"You owe me a dollar. Pay up!"

7: EDDIE THE CHAMP

I am a *man,* Eddie Campanaro thought, without doing a thing to prove his manhood.

Stolidly, he stood, thick and wide, swarthy, a onetime United States Marine who'd earned a Bronze Star in Korea.

So, okay, he was getting along, close to forty. No matter. House captain, that was his job. He ran the whole friggin' show. *No* sumbitch got past the door of Don Cafu's pad without Eddie The Champ's okay, the old Mark I eyeball inspection. Day, night, frig it. Four o'clock in the morning, zero four hundred hours, they used to call it in the Crotch.

That's one of the things Eddie The Champ remembered most vividly about the Marine Corps. Salty bunch of dudes, *men,* but with a capacity to laugh at themselves: USMC, Uncle Sam's Moldy Crotch. The outcasts. Hadn't Cinch himself said so, Truman. Commander In Chief.

That's what Eddie The Champ remembered, after

twenty years. Champ of what? Okay, he had hands. Golden Gloves. A winner. Then the dough. Seventeen pro fights, then six main events. He won two. He drew two, both fixed. He got the crap kicked out of himself running in against a rawboned awkward redhead with freckled shoulders from some busher dump. Omaha? Where the hell was Omaha? Dumbass kid didn't have half Eddie's class, smoothness, style, moves. All he could do was hit like a mule kicking, even his awkward left jab, and Jeez-ussss . . . those right-hand shots to the body. Eddie caved in during the third, and the hick from Omaha splattered Eddie's fine, beaked Roman nose all over Eddie's face, and he woke up on the table with an ammonia inhaler under his nose.

Sure, lucky punch, everyone said so, crumbum from Hicksville. But, god, what a whanging right hand. Eddie felt sore and as though he breathed glass for three weeks afterwards.

The second Main he went against some long-limbed spade with a fancy monicker like Jolmo Bantuli, some such shit, a *cause* type. Eddie fancied him around a half-dozen rounds, flicking left, rocking the spade's head doubling, sometimes tripling combinations, so far ahead on points the judges got restless, yawning. Christ, Eddie The Champ thought, where's it been all my life, this kind of easy dough? Main event. He snapped three fast lefts into the spade's blunt nose, crossed with a right, dropped his shoulder and shoveled two fast left hooks, just a fraction low, into the black hide. Then Jolmo came up with that dynamite right cross and he went blind.

One punch.

Eddie The Champ almost died right in the ring. His jaw was broken in five places and unhinged below his left ear. He had a severe concussion where the back of his head smashed into the canvas. He lay in hospital nine weeks, soup through a glass straw, then finely strained baby food. He had a lot of time to think. The main thing he thought was fuck fighting. He wanted no more dumbutt hicks from Omaha, or funny-named blacks from Kenya. He wanted good, uncomplicated, steady work requiring no great physical effort and a good payday, preferably tax free.

In those days just after the Korean War, the early to late fifties, all fighting on the East Coast was totally "mobbed up." Sometimes a guy won, other times he took a fall, and occasionally the bout was completely square. So long as the bout went at least five rounds, so the TV guys got in all their commercials and ad-agency people kept happy, what the hell?

Okay, sure, they sent the mob guy to the joint, finally. He rigged too many fights, kept the ad-agency boys too happy.

Eddie The Champ could care less. He was out of it then, back home upriver, taking on a little weight, moving from a natural welter to light-heavy, then heavy. He could put a hell of a shot behind 200 pounds holding a short length of lead pipe convincing some factory dumbutt the vigorish had to be paid, never mind the principal.

Eddie never remembered quite how or why.

He got a little too eager, had a trifle more enthusiasm than necessary, or had perhaps just gained too much weight. He leaned into the muscle too hard, and "the arm" as the Mafia was called in his part of New York State, was out one customer and had a killer on its hands.

The commission met. Eddie expected death, unless the contingency plan he worked out did work out. And then he found himself alive, forgiven, pockets stuffed full of cash, passport, documentation, and a singular assignment.

Go "home."

Recruit an army.

Train them. Make *soldiers* of them.

Then turn them over to Don Cafu. He knows the rest.

And one hell of a job it was, too! Beautiful. He had guys beating down his door to join up. He had booze, babes, a bunk five feet wide, and never enjoyed any of them! He found himself not only recruiter, screening officer, training officer, and troop commander, but Don Cafu's house captain. Only by luck did he escape the yardboss job. Fortunately, Don Cafu had a long-time totally trusted retainer who watched the estate grounds, with a crew of locals and several studs who'd finally lost the last-ditch battle with the U. S. Immigration Service and gotten shipped "home."

During his *easy* life in the Sicilian province of Agrigento, Eddie The Champ had lost forty-three pounds. None of his expensive New York tailoring fit. He felt strong as a bull and horny as a billygoat. When he got time to lie awake and think about women, it lasted perhaps three minutes after he awoke at dawn, until Don Cafu pressed the buzzer that rasped like an angry wasp in Eddie The Champ Campanaro's ear.

Eddie bounded from his old-fashioned bed with the five-foot-high hand-carved headboard and mashed the button on the intercom, this particular dawn in late spring. "Yeah, Chief, I'm awake."

"Get down here, *now!*"

"Okay, Chief, soon as I finish washing my face, and I gotta shave."

The old man spoke English quite well. He was another of the deportees, years past; but when anger and passion overtook him, he fell back into his mother tongue, and Campanaro could hardly follow the cursing, shouting, absolute commands, so much slang, some of it *omerta* stuff, the forbidden language. Except to those inside.

Campanaro got off the bed and lit a cigarette, coughed, poured a huge handpainted crockery basin full of tepid water, dropped a thin washcloth into the water, then hooked an equally fancy large jar from under his bed.

A ton of money the old bastard must have, Campanaro thought, a *ton*—weigh it! Renting soldiers out to Frankie Angeletti for a thousand clams a day! Got to be big stakes to afford that kind of overhead.

Sicily. Home. Rich. Respected. Feared. And you want to take a leak, what do you do? Pull a jar out from under the goddam bed. Or walk a hundred yards out back. Christ. Like friggin' Korea!

Campanaro did his business, then turned to the basin beside the large pitcher and washed quickly, smeared his face with soap and ran his double-edged razor over his light beard. Swarthy or not, he was lucky in that respect. He had no blue jaw with grainy stickers sprouting an hour after shaving.

He dressed hurriedly in native clothing, all he had that now fit him. He tied his trousers up with a thin cord, slipped his feet into rope-soled sandals and headed for the door as the intercom rasped again, like an angry wasp.

8: AGRIGENTO ANGUISH

Don Cafu stopped pacing and stared at Eddie The Champ. "Well, well, you got nothing to say? You gonna stare till the words drop off the paper?"

Eddie shrugged, flapping the long eight-page radiogram. The whole thing was in an open code of which Eddie understood perhaps a tenth. Christ, it was like Navajo, for which there was no alphabet, no written language. That's why the Marines used Navajos for radio telephone operators during the Pacific war and in Korea. Even when the gooks intercepted a transmission, loud and clear, five by five, they got nothing but gibberish. How can you write down something that don't exist on paper, but is only noise?

The old greaseballs had the same kind of thing, but they had over the years worked out a phonetic phraseology, which they kept to themselves. In all the world, Eddie figured, maybe fifty guys knew enough of the "language" to read the radiogram.

"Hah! Some goddam house captain I got!" Don Cafu snarled. "What if I'm not here when this came in, hah? What about that?"

"Chief, I can't help not knowing," Eddie said. "You old guys—"

"Now you calling me a greaseball, hah? My own house *capo*? You go ahead, tough guy. Try it. Then you be a grease *spot*! I throw gasoline on you, a match, *phoof!* And like you never existed. Gone, a puff of stinking smoke."

"Okay, Chief, okay. That still don't tell me anything except what we already know. I don't dig." Eddie waved the radiogram. "You want me to know, you got to tell me. It's not doing any good yelling at me because I don't read your secret codes."

Don Cafu whirled on Eddie, hooded brown, reptilian eyes flashing with anger, and then he stopped, sighed, let his shoulders sag. He shuffled across the tiled floor and patted Eddie on the arm. "You're right, Eddie. You're a good boy and you're right. My anger I'm taking out on you. Here, sit down, have a cup of coffee, and maybe some brandy. There's a chill in the air this morning."

Eddie felt no chill. He felt sweat under his chin and along his flanks. He sat down at the round old-fashioned hand-carved table, facing the don. He spread the radiogram on the white cloth. Don Cafu poured coffee for them both, slurped noisily, opened a bottle of *grappa*, refilled the cup and stirred with his finger. Eddie thought, the table manners of these old greaseballs would gag a buzzard.

Don Cafu slurped again, put his cup down and jerked his chin at the radiogram. "What it says is no more seventy-five thousand bucks a day rental for our soldiers, Eddie."

"What! Some son of a bitch's crossing us! That goddam Frankie!"

The don quieted Eddie with a gesture. "Don't curse the dead. It's bad luck."

"Dead? Wha—"

Don Cafu gestured again, and Eddie fell silent. "You know of this Mack Bolan, this Executioner he calls himself?"

"You ain't telling me *one* guy took out seventy-five of our best, Chief." Eddie shook his head. "Excuse me, boss, with all respect, but that's bullshit. No *way!* I personally *trained* those guys. Physical conditioning, weapons, stealth, fire and maneuver." Eddie flicked the radiogram, shaking his head. "If that's what this says, somebody's putting a shuck on you, Chief, trying to cross you, work our soldiers without paying."

"You a good boy, Eddie. I like you. But you got a mouth on you gonna get you killed one day, you don't learn." Don Cafu smiled; he looked like a death mask. "This came from *The* Man. You understand me, Eddie, *capo di tutti capi?*"

"Boss of bosses."

"That's right, Eddie. So no more about a shuck, hah? No more about stealing our soldiers or bullshit, hah?"

"Okay, okay, I'm sorry. So what happened, and please, Chief, don't tell me this Bolan cat wiped out seventy-five of our best."

"Kill them all? No. I think he killed only about thirty, personally, you understand? But how you like that, hah? One man, thirty deads! The rest, they kill each other or now in jail."

"And Frankie, our payday?"

"This you listen close, Eddie. The commission sent a wild card hit-man to Philly, an expert, the *best*. And you know what happens? I tell you, listen close. This bastard Bolan takes the hit man—" Don Cafu snapped his fingers like a gunshot "—and sells *him* to Frankie as himself. You understand?"

"Jesus Christ in all His truth!"

"Hah? That's right. You know what else he does, Eddie. He collects the bounty on himself, this bastard Bolan. One hundred and ten of the Large. That was *our* money, Eddie."

"You mean for the soldiers we sent, all the expense we had training them, getting them smuggled in . . . we get *nothing?*"

"You a smart boy, Eddie. You catch on fast."

"That stupid Frankie, I—"

"No, not the dead, don't curse the dead boy, bad luck."

"Bolan got him, too."

"No, the commission took care of Frankie."

"What! Goddam, Chief, you got me going in circles."

"A good lesson you should learn. *Don't panic!* That's what happened in Philly, and the *commissione,* too, I'm sorry to say. Frankie took the head in to collect the bounty. The commission thought he was trying to pull a fast one, rolling out the hit-man's head, claiming it was Bolan. So no more Frankie Angeletti, no more Don Stefano Angeletti, no more Outfit in Philly, because they panicked."

"And Bolan? Just walked out?" Eddie buried his face in his hands, anguish like physical pain as he closed his eyes and thought of all the months of grinding hard work he'd put into training his soldiers, the arrangements, expenses, and now all gone, a fart in a whirlwind. Key-*rist!*

Eddie became aware of Don Cafu's voice. He raised his face and looked at the old man. The don poured again. "Here, more coffee, and now, hah? You want a slug of brandy?"

"Hell, yes!"

"Okay, help yourself," and Eddie did as the don spoke. "No, Bolan did not just walk out. Number one, he was

70

shot to pieces, Naturally, we hoped he'd die. But one of our *amicu di l'amici,* you know, friend of friends, a transit cop, he spotted the hit-man's Maserati coming into The City. He made a call. The New York people knew Bolan had a doctor he sometimes used and they got to the doctor before Bolan did, made him an offer he couldn't refuse, hah?" Don Cafu grinned like a shark. He slurped more brandied coffee, then banged down his cup in anger. "But the bastard got away, even after the doc gave him a hit that should have knocked nine mules flat."

Don Cafu raised a hand and pointed at Eddie The Champ. "You *understand* this, hah? This is a *tough* bastard we're dealing with. Not movie tough, not some old gangster picture, Edward G. Robinson or Cagney growling from the side of his mouth, hah? Tough, this guy. Tough, Eddie, you hear."

"Yeah, okay, I hear, Chief," Eddie said, puzzled. "So he's a real badass. What does it mean to us?"

"It means, you dumb shit, I've been telling you all this for a reason! You think I talk for my health, hah? For exercise? He's coming *here.* Now you understand, hah? Clear now? You *got* it? You goddam dumbhead!" In fury, the old don slammed his fist down on the table so hard the cup jumped from its saucer, fell sideways, rolled off and shattered on the tile floor. "HERE!"

"Shit, he ain't got a chance," Eddie said. And to his astonishment, Don Cafu began laughing. But it was a bitter, anguished, coarsely grinding laugh, totally devoid of humor.

"Eddie, you a good boy. I like, I always liked you. But you keep thinking like that, and I don't like you no more so much, hah? No use liking a dead man."

Stupefied, Eddie The Champ stared at his don.

Don Cafu rose to his feet and lumbered heavily on arthritic feet to a vast sideboard, found a glass, blew dust from it, returned to his chair and poured a generous slug of *grappa*. He took a swallow, sighed and licked his lips.

"Yeah, Eddie, keep thinking this Bolan bastard ain't got a chance coming here!" The don slammed his fist down again. "And I need a new house captain."

Eddie raised his hands, "But, Christ, boss. How? I mean, this guy's wanted everywhere. How the hell's he going to cross the goddam ocean, get through immigration and customs?"

"Goddam, you Eddie," the don raged, "get it through your head. This guy's got balls like a water buffalo, and he's *smart*. What you think, hah? He walks into La Guardia wearing a ton of heat and tries to catch TWA to Rome?"

The don's voice suddenly quieted, became lethal in its toneless flat hissing. "This guy you say ain't got a chance has already blown up more than a thousand soldiers. He went through Boston like a tank over a baby carriage, exposed a guy it took twelve years to plant in society and top-echelon government. He took over the Angeletti house in Philly. He *slept* there. After he escaped from the doctor, he destroyed two more soldiers who had the car staked out, then he dropped off the face of the earth for nine days, vanished. Then turns up at Teterboro airport and charters a private jet. Another of our friends gets word to us, but not in time, hah? So we can send guns after him, just one of our girls planted at the airport, a hustler but also a spotter for unguarded freight. She's at the bottom of the goddam ocean, sharkbait. The jet lands at the Azores, gets a plate riveted over the open window, refuels, and for all I know the son of a bitch is circling overhead this minute ready to make a napalm run on my house!"

Don Cafu smashed his fist down on the table. "You still think so, hah? He ain't got a chance, this Bolan bastard? Answer me, you idiot!"

"Okay, boss, okay," Eddie The Champ said, bottom falling from his guts.

"Okay, okay, what, hah?" The don grabbed his glass and drained the last big gulp of grappa. "Get your dumb ass outside and get to *work!*"

9: NEAPOLITAN NIGHTMARE

Mack Bolan knew that *Mafia,* both the word and the original organization bearing the name, originated in Sicily. The so-called Castellammarese War ripped open the Italian underworld in the early 1930s, littering the streets of various cities in the U.S. with more than sixty deads, and an unknown number of others simply vanished.

The outcome of this mutually destructive warfare resulted in settling once and for all the question of Sicilian versus mainland Italian—particularly Neapolitan—dominance of the Italian-American underworld.

The emergence of two men as Number One and Number Two, Charley Lucky Luciano, a Sicilian, and Vito Genovese from Naples, allied and working together and ruling with steel-fisted discipline, ordered the traditional factions to stop feuding and fighting for dominance, and all come together into "this thing of ours": the *Cosa Nostra.*

For Mack Bolan, as for most people not members of a

Family, the terms were, and are, interchangeable. Mafia
. . . Cosa Nostra.

And The Executioner did not deal in semantics, in
vague shadings of word definitions. He had set out on
another mission against the Mafia, this time to turn the
Mafia's soldier training school into hell ground, and he
was well on his way.

After Bolan shot the window out and the girl went,
Captain Teaf shoved the nose down and put the chartered jet on the deck, calling a MAYDAY. He wanted to
turn back, but Bolan/Borzi refused.

"Christ, man," Teaf shouted, "we won't have ten minutes reserve fuel over the Azores. We miss one approach
or have to hold, and we ditch, right into the drink!"

"Then you'd better not foul things up, huh? What do
you think the bonus was for? You've got the uniform and
the shoulder boards and big gold-plated wings, so let's
see if you're a pilot!"

Teaf remembered that TWA had not thought so, and
had dismissed him before his probationary period ended;
that's how he ended up scrambling for nickles and dimes
around dead-end country airports, until he'd smuggled in
some "items" and got a good payday which allowed him
to finance himself and get his airline transport rating.
Armed with the Big Ticket, he found better jobs easier
to get, and now he held the best he'd ever have. If he
lived.

Like most executive and airline pilots, Teaf privately
admitted he was overpaid, most of the time. But things
had a way of catching up, so about twice a year on the
average a professional pilot found himself in a position
where he would have been willing to trade places with
almost any other man in the world. Even a convict serving time could reasonably look forward to eventual free-
dom, and life.

Teaf looked at the big ice-eyed bastard sitting in the

right seat and knew this one of those times when he would earn it all, the bonus and more.

Once satisfied the pilot was continuing on course, Bolan went back into the cabin. Even though down on the deck, perhaps 200 feet above the wave-tops and the warm air, a chill had invaded the cabin. For even though Teaf had pulled back the power to conserve fuel at the low altitude, the jet's speed still exceeded 300 knots, and wind whistled through the destroyed window with hurricane force.

Bolan examined the cabin for a few moments. Then he slipped the catches on the sliding metal door on the built-in bar. He carried the two-by-three piece of polished duraluminum back to the open window, righted the seats the girl had made into a bed, then wedged the bardoor between the tops of two seats, covering the hole.

The wind still howled and buffeted through the remaining cracks, but the chill and noise diminished greatly. Mack found a cabinet holding more linen, pillows, cushions, and crammed them into the cracks, further cutting the wind and sound. Then he found the access door to the çargo hold and went down inside.

His crate had been opened, yeah. And more. Until now Bolan had felt bad, real bad, felt like hell about the girl, killing women wasn't in his line.

But he discovered now *she* had been playing for keeps. The crate was booby trapped. It took him more than half an hour of sweating effort to disarm the simple devices. That was what one-time professional soldier Mack Bolan had never ceased marveling at, and putting to use.

The simple plans worked. The simple devices. Start jacking around with complicated procedures, super secret agent stuff, and first thing you knew, one of your own men got blown up. He forgot, or became nervous, sweaty, hurried, the timing failed to work out or the wire went

77

slack in an unseasonal waft of warm air. The only guys you screwed when you made it fancy were yourselves.

Finished, Mack Bolan went back to the cockpit. "How we doing?"

"Twenty minutes out. I've called an emergency and we are first to land, a straight-in approach."

Bolan saw the pilot flick a glance his way. "Thanks to you, we're fat on fuel. Plugging that hole was smart."

"I got cold back there."

"Yeah, sure." Teaf knew Borzi had spent the better part of an hour in the cargo hold. He'd felt it in the controls. Shifting over two hundred pounds that far aft, and the two hundred pound man moving around. Teaf had kept his thumb on the electric trim button on the control wheel, compensating for the shifts in weight back aft.

Bolan sat in the cockpit's right seat during the landing. As he anticipated but dreaded, there were too many people—firemen with their trucks and foam hoses, cops, a crowd of gawkers, airport officials, and as they taxied in and Teaf shut down the engines, Bolan said, "Don't forget what the bonus is for, ace. And there's more to come."

The pilot earned his money. Bolan was hardly bothered. In forty minutes Teaf had arranged for an aluminum plate to be solidly riveted over the hole left by the window. Fortunately, a wide blood-red stripe ran down the length of the airplane along the same line as the spaced windows, and if they noticed anything untoward, the ground engineers said nothing.

While the mechanics worked, the line crew refueled the jet, and in less than two hours after landing Teaf lifted the jet off the runway again, eastbound. At Bolan's instructions, he'd taken on a maximum load of fuel and recharged all ox-cylinders, so in case the cabin failed to pressurize with the patch, they could still fly at high altitude and get maximum performance from the jet engines. The patch held though both men kept their masks dangling around their necks. Also, on Bolan's orders, Teaf had filed direct for Naples, some 2,200 miles, well within the jet's range if the weather held and the met-guys at Azores said it should be clear sailing all the way.

Once airborne and the ship on flight director, with Teaf relaxing in his shoved-back seat, Bolan peeled off another $1000 and tossed it into the pilot's lap. "You did a good job, ace."

Teaf nodded and folded the money into his shirt pocket. "If you're sweating Napoli, the crate and all—forget it. I sent a radiogram while we were on the deck at the island. The fix is in."

The hair on Bolan's neck bristled. *Which* fix, he wondered. Getting the crate past customs, or waxing Mack Bolan's ass?

The Mike Borzi cover had to be blown by now, because the girl had known. Or had she? Maybe not. It was just possible she had only recognized him, but had no time.

And she had not seen Mack's phony passport. No way. Only she had disrobed.

Bolan looked around the cockpit. He saw latches and handles on the windows on each side of the cockpit. "Do these open?"

"Hold on, man!" Teaf shouted.

"I'm not touching anything," Bolan said. "Do they?"

"Sure. Just slip the catch," Teaf put his finger on the latch beside his face, "then pull back. Nothing to it."

Bolan looked at the window. Open, it would give him a firing port about eighteen inches by almost two feet. The nose of the airplane sloped down sharply, giving him an open view forward. The wings were placed at a mid-fuselage position, well behind the cockpit and high enough so he could see well back under them. From the cockpit, if necessary, he had something close to 300-degree vision.

From directly behind would be the only safe place for an attacker to approach.

But as they flew onwards, toward the east, first raising the coast of Portugal, then the snow-tipped Pyrénées along the French-Spanish frontier, Bolan liked bullassing straight into Naples less and less.

The radiogram . . . .

Professional soldier Mack Bolan knew no better way to insure suicide than notifying the enemy of your coming.

And to die in Naples would be stupid. It would be like a race driver dying in a freeway wreck. Naples had but one purpose. Diversion.

Dead men divert nothing, no one, and achieve no main objective.

Bolan's left hand flashed out and took Teaf's throat. "Let's see the copy."

Wind clamped off, voice-box almost crushed, Teaf could not speak, only point. Except he did not point. He pounded his shirt pocket. Bolan found the flimsy paper, released the pilot.

PERSONAL . . . INSPECTOR G. LISA, CUS-TOMS CONTROL, NAPLES INTERNATION-AL AIRPORT . . . ESTIMATED TIME ARRIVAL EIGHTEEN HUNDRED THIRTY HOURS ZULU . . . ONE VIP WITH PERSON-AL EFFECTS . . . DESIRES ANONYMITY IDENTICAL HOWARD HUGHES WITH SAME ABILITY PAY EXPEDITIOUS TREAT-MENT . . . ENDS . . . TEAF.

It worked.

Bolan had no choice but to ride along, not being a pilot. And evidently, Customs Officer Lisa held consider-able power, because when Teaf notified Naples approach control sixty miles out, he was given a vector that set the jet up for a straight-in approach. Upon the hand-over to Tower, the controller directed Teaf to land at once, take the second hispeed turnoff and proceed directly to ramp area Bravo. Once off the runway, Teaf tuned his radio to ground control and the instructions were repeated. He halted the jet before a small, single-story building, isolated from the rest of the terminal complex, and as Teaf shut down, a single man came striding purposefully from the building. He wore a uniform, a Sam Browne type military harness—wide leather belt with narrow shoulder strap, and on the belt hung a holstered pistol. The holster flap was down and snapped in place.

Teaf had depressurized as they taxied in, so the door popped open easily when he turned the handle and lowered it, steps unfolding. The uniformed officer came immediately aboard, stopped just inside the cabin, clacked his booted heels, bowed slightly, and touched a finger to the glossy brim of his cap. "Ah, yes, *Capitano!*"

Teaf stepped forward and shook hands with Inspector Lisa. Bolan saw a flash of green.

And that was it. That easy. Bolan kept waiting for the hook, for the kink in the line, the catch; but none came. An old truck stood waiting beside the small building. In ten minutes the driver had Bolan's crate aboard and roped down, Bolan's papers had been processed—customs, immigration, public health, the works. Bolan pulled the pilot aside. "The only thing I want you to remember about me is that we can do business again if it goes this well."

Teaf held out his hand, palm up.

Good enough, Bolan thought. I wouldn't trust him if he wanted to be pals, go have a drink, now we're past the heat. All he wants is his pay for work done. Bolan paid him and climbed into the truck with the driver.

Carlo Maligno stood in the window of his office and looked across the Bay of Naples. He saw none of the internationally famous splendor which drew hundreds of thousands of tourists each year, from all over the world. He saw but one thing, and chewed his cigar with satisfaction. In the deepening gloom of sundown, he saw the lights ablaze at dockside where the U.S. freighter S.S. *Sundance* lay tied to, hatches open, cargo booms working. Carlo had finally broken down the ship's skipper, some dumbutt spic from Brownsville, Texas, who thought the unloading charges too high.

Carlo grunted. Too high! *He* thought. Spics weren't supposed to think, only pay, through the nose. And both ears, if Carlo Maligno said. Carlo wasn't boss of the docks for nothing, and not for his health. And he didn't keep shiploads of perishables standing by out of meanness, either. It was a simple matter of economics. If the ship's owners wanted the vegetables unloaded and sold in Italy, then they paid. So what? It jacked up the street price, and the poor went without greens, let'm eat cake! The room behind Carlo darkened, as though someone had stepped into the doorway and blocked the light.

Carlo turned, "Hey, get outta—" His voice died in his throat and he tasted a vile bitterness as he bit his cigar in half and the soggy wet end lodged halfway down his gullet.

The man in the door stood over six feet tall and wore a black commando uniform. The man's left hand moved and a small piece of metal sailed across the room, landing at Carlo Maligno's feet. Entranced, Carlo looked down, and in the dim light he saw what he recognized as a marksmanship badge from the days when the Yanks came through during the Big War. Then Carlo went blind, because The Executioner shot him through the top of the head.

Twenty minutes later, as Vassallo Flaccido sat in his

tilted-back chair outside the garbage collectors' union hall, guarding the door because the bosses had a meeting going, so they could raise the rates again, Vassallo suddenly found himself sitting in mid-air. He landed hard on his fat rump, shook his head and stared up, felt his overworked heart pump too hard and a ripping pain shoot across his chest and down his left arm when his eyes saw the huge man in black with the gun in his hand.

Bolan stepped over the coronary case, opened the door, went catlike up the union-hall steps, opened the door and stepped inside. Only one light in the room, bright, a chipped green shade over it. The garbage union bosses conducted their meetings with considerable style and minimum formality. Six men sat around a poker table covered with green velvet. On side trays stood bottles and glasses, coldcuts, sliced fresh vegetables. Vivace Lena briskly riffled the cards, shuffled them, offered them for a cut, began dealing a hand of five-card draw poker. When the cards were out, Lena put the deck down and placed a coin atop it. "Okay, who opens?"

A metallic object came out of the gloom beyond the hanging light and landed with a smack, dead-center in the table. Then a flat, toneless voice said, "I open, and play the hand I've got."

Bolan got Lena through the forehead first shot, then ticked off three more as they froze for a moment before bursting into frantic action. Bolan opened the door and backed out, flipped a grenade, then leaped down the stairs. He was almost a half-block away when the delay-fuse set the grenade off and blew out every window in the upstairs room, killing the last two bosses.

One man survived the attack long enough to make a telephone call, but the man he called did not believe him. He laughed, said, "You're drunk again, Immondo," and hung up. He rolled back over and placed his dark, black-furred paw on the blonde's vast bosom. Jeeez-usss, thought

Vistoso Mezzano, there's nothing like these Kraut and Dane and Swede babes, once our Corsican pals get them tamed down and broken in!

The girl's milk-white skin still showed faint bruise marks, and high inside one thigh the cigarette burn scars had healed but still showed plainly. This one said her name was Hilde and she had gone to Paris with her sister on vacation, the both of them school teachers in Bavaria, and one night a truly distinguished looking but slightly threadbare man offered to guide them on a tour: those parts of Paris the ordinary visitor never saw. Of course it wasn't dangerous, what a thought! And they could take pictures, too—eh? Eh? They went first to a dingy place full of hashish smoke, stinking of sweat and vomit, and watched a pair of Apache dancers abuse one another, then to another place where other women and some men sat around a large glass. Some of them had cameras. When Hilde sat down she could see that under the glass was a room. In the room was a bed. On the bed lay a man and two women. Hilde watched in astonished fascination for a moment, then got to her feet, held onto the back of her chair, and asked her guide, please, for a glass of water, she felt so faint. She awoke with a crushing sick headache, and cottony mouth turned wrong-side out. She lay sick, thirsty, hungry, cold, and terrified for what seemed days, until an incredibly cruel little man, hardly five feet tall, came for her. She had not believed such pain as the little man could inflict truly existed. She had been brought up on the myth that God provided His children with an automatic cutout device, so that when pain became unendurable, you became unconscious. Once she learned this an absolute falsehood, her training began . . . and now here she was, hoping *Signor* Mezzano would be good to her because she had graduated with honors and could make the *signor* very, very

84

happy. No, she had never seen her sister again, since that night in Paris, why?

Mezzano giggled and buried his face between the vast pillowy milk-white bosoms, and he suddenly felt Hilde's entire body grow tense, then stiff as a corpse.

Mezzano raised up. "Hey, that's no way to be nice."

He saw her face. The total terror in her unblinking green eyes. Mezzano whirled around and looked up at the man in black. The man in black thrust out his hand, and Mezzano automatically accepted the proffered object. He stared at it. What the hell? It had the shape of a Formée Cross. A bar across the bottom read MARKSMAN.

Recognition came in an instant to Mezzano and he lunged back, trying to squirm beneath the girl, and death forever darkened the light. He heard a faint *phutt* and felt a millisecond of pain, then nothing.

By the time he left Mezzano's establishment, The Executioner left a total of ten deads.

Before midnight Bolan hit another union boss and his underbosses, leaving six dead in a central-city private dining room, and leaving the Neapolitan teamsters leaderless. He struck the waterfront numbers bank, doubled back, destroyed all the betting slips and set fire to the *lira*. He destroyed every last vehicle of a car rental agency which had been taken over by Mafia through extortion and terror. On the outskirts of the city he blew up a Mafia-owned bank which the feds had learned did most of the financing of international smuggling operations between Italy and the U.S.

At midnight, The Executioner made a telephone call: "Get your women out of the house."

In panic, the Naples *Capo di tutti Capi,* Boss of Bosses, fled with his women and most of his retinue, and Bolan virtually destroyed the Frode estate with his most recent acquisition, an M79 grenade launcher. Much lighter and more portable than a bazooka, it also had the advantage of not gushing out a huge black-blast of flame and dust when fired. True, it did not have the knock-down penetration power of a rocket launcher, but with practice, and The Executioner had gotten plenty in Nam, he could put one frag after another through doors and windows from maximum range.

Shortly after eight o'clock the following morning, two events occurred almost simultaneously. First, a non-union truck driver/owner who had barely managed to feed his large family for the past six years, carried a lighted lamp into a closet, pulled the door shut and locked it, and then counted the money again, just to be sure. It had not been a dream. The peculiar big man with the eyes that ran shivers up Fretta's back really had bought Fretta's ancient truck, for cash, in U.S. dollars, and paid more than a new Italian model would cost. He *knew* dealing with that customs man would pay off some day, and it had!

At the same time, on a dusty road a hundred miles down the peninsula, in Calabria not far south of Castro-vallari, a big man in worn clothing, face grimy, cap pulled low over his ice-blue eyes, drove an old rattling truck with a crate lashed down behind the cab. The Executioner took a bite of the moldy cheese he'd bought just after dawn from a farmer's wife on the road. He washed the cheese down with some bitter-tasting native wine. Perhaps when he reached Reggio, at the toe of the boot, just across the Strait of Messina from his objective, Bolan would feel safe. Yeah, safe.

But so far his deaf-mute act had worked, buying gasoline, the food and wine, never dismounting from the truck except, on deserted stretches of road, to check the oil and water levels of the truck's engine. The last thing he could afford to do in the vast, sparsely populated, desert-like regions of Calabria was put himself afoot so he had to depend upon other people, other transport.

He nursed the old truck along, and wondered if he

dare use the ferry across the Strait to Sicily. In the meantime, Bolan allowed himself a wry smile. He couldn't expect it to work every time, but hopefully his nightmarish multiple strikes in Naples had set off another internal war among the dons and bosses and soldiers, especially the ambitious ones left fighting for control of the unions Bolan had left without bosses.

"Have fun, boys," The Executioner muttered aloud, and took another sip of bitter wine.

10: A TABLE FOR THE DON

To *mafiosi,* a nation at war, particularly their own country, is meaningless. Except that warfare invariably provides them with increased opportunities for illicit profits, most frequently black-marketing those items which became rationed: gasoline, meat, flour, sugar, liquor, auto tires, shoes.

Mafiosi, members of "this thing of ours" owe a higher, overriding allegiance, to which they have given a blood oath, and into which they were born.

This heritage, tradition, and membership both requires and molds a certain mentality, so that Don Vito Genovese, Mafia ruler of southern Italy, headquartered in Naples, could not believe it when he was arrested by a U.S. Army CID agent in 1944. His disbelief became speechless, staggering incredulity when Sergeant O. C. Dickey flatly refused a $250,000 cash bribe and personally returned Genovese to the U.S. in 1945, to face trial for murder.

Into this sudden power vacuum, several Neapolitan underbosses moved, and with their crews fell into internal warfare for control until Charley Lucky Luciano, who had been released from a New York penitentiary, was deported from the States and came home to straighten things out. After Luciano's death and another inner struggle, Don Tronfio Frode emerged as Boss of all Bosses.

But after The Executioner's nightmarish strike in Napoli, the few surviving dons, and the capos who instantly seized power upon learning of their bosses' deaths, called "a table."

In a word, the Naples boss of bosses found himself on *trial*.

From Rome, from Genoa, from Reggio and the Sicilian provinces, the dons came, and they all came with the same question on their lips: "What the fuck is going on here, can't you control your own Family?"

"Listen to me, this wasn't Family, you get that? *Not* Family!"

"Then what?" demanded Brinato from Rome in an icy voice.

"That bastard Bolan, the one they call The Executioner."

"Bullshit," said Vandalo from Palermo. "One guy blowing up a whole town. Bullshit."

Frode turned his head and looked at Vandalo; his upper lip twisted with contempt, as though Vandalo were something in a test tube from the VD lab. "Where the hell you been, and doing what? Hustling dope again, and shooting your own stuff?"

"Listen, you bastard!"

"No, *you* listen, all of you!" Frode shouted. "Bolan, that bastard Bolan." He pointed a thrusting finger at Vandalo, then at Brinato, the ice-cold bastard. "Any of you notice anything, here, this table you called on me?"

All the dons looked around at one another. Vicercato, the foppishly overdressed don from Catania suddenly popped his forehead with the heel of his hand. "Hey! Hee—ey! Where the hell is Cafu, huh?"

"Yeah," Frode snarled, voice peeling hide from these creeps who dared call a table on him. "Where the hell is Cafu?" His voice mocked Vicercato.

The other dons looked at one another, and shifted uncomfortably. Frode felt his presence and counterattack regaining control of the situation. "You guys are nuts, if you think Bolan can't take down a whole goddam town, *any* town. You don't believe me, get in touch with what's left of the Angeletti outfit in Philly, huh? Or Boston. Huh? Is it coming back to you dumb bastards now? Is it?"

Frode leaned back in his chair and lit a fat Cuban cigar. The other dons looked at one another, and began muttering to themselves. Frode let them talk for a moment while he got the cigar going well, then he slapped his palm down on the big polished table. "This is the guy, *the* guy, one guy, Bolan, a single man, who flew right into Glass Bay, Puerto Rico where we had a million fucking soldiers waiting for him. And all he did was blow up Vince Triesta's house, crashed an airplane into it, took down the hardsite, wiped out that thing of ours, the Caribbean Carousel."

Frode turned his head and deliberately spat on the thick, expensive carpet. "You pricks make me sick."

"And you make me sick," a gravelly voice said from behind Frode. The don froze, cigar falling from his trembling fingers. He knew the voice. It was that of his house boss, Astio Traditore.

Frode swallowed heavily, jumped to his feet and whirled, shouting. "Get out! You don't belong here. This is a table for dons."

"Then you don't belong either, *Don* Tronfio," Astio said, twisting the title obscenely.

Big, swarthy, dressed in immaculate Italian silk tailoring and custom-lasted shoes from London, Astio stepped forward.

"You know something, *boss*," again the snotty twist to the word, "the only thing a don has going for him is respect. Whether the respect comes from fear, from good treatment, from letting us have our own things inside this big thing of ours, a don stays a don because his lieutenants and his soldiers respect him."

Astio Traditore spat at Frode's feet. "I don't respect no son of a bitch who cuts and runs with the women when someone tries to take down his hardsite."

Astio shifted his attention to the sharklike faces around the table for Don Tronfio Frode. "One of the first out the door. Look at him. Cut and scratched all to hell, running through the groves, hiding. Came crawling back in after daylight this morning, rumpled and dirty, like a fucking hound with his tail between his legs. I got no more respect for this pile of guts, and I don't work for no man I don't respect."

In his chilled voice, Brinato from Rome said, "You're taking over? Is that what you're telling the table?"

"I'm *telling* the table nothing," Astio said, with just the right touch of humility, "except I can't work for him no longer. I'm taking myself and my crews out. I'm open to offers."

Brinato gestured. "Bring a chair, join the table."

After Traditore seated himself, Brinato said, "We discuss the other in a moment. First I want to know, we all want to know, was it Bolan?"

Without hesitation, Traditore shook his head: no.

"Lie!" Don Frode shouted. "Look, goddammit, LOOK!" He threw three marksman badges on the table. "The trademark—The Executioner's trademark."

The table remained silent, each don looking at the badges, then at Frode, finally shifting their gazes to Astio Traditore.

Astio smoothed his silk jacket, bent his thick lips in a slight smile, and said, "Dime store garbage. Anybody want a ton of them, tomorrow, this evening after dinner? I can get a good price on a trainload of that crap, all just alike."

"You lousy goddam traitor!" Frode screamed. "All I done for you, a rotten goddam punk pimping your sister to American sailors, and I brought you in like a son, and now you stab me, cut my throat. *Traitor!*"

Astio looked at Frode, his face totally without expression, and then after a moment, he nodded. "For respect. When I respected you, anything. Anything." Astio made a gesture as though brushing aside a fly. "No more."

"Just a minute now," said the Catania boss. "We're not taking down no don on this kind of evidence. First, I want to hear someone else besides this boy here say that our friend ran out last night. Then I want other witnesses, like what the hell? Somebody must have seen this Bolan if he blew up the city like our friend Frode claims."

"No witnesses," Frode said helplessly. "He took everyone down each place he hit." He gestured at the metal objects on the table. "There's your evidence. That's his goddam MO, all of you know it."

"And we know the kid is right, too. Anybody could make the hits and leave that crap behind, to blame Bolan, you agree?" Brinato looked at the other faces for confirmation.

"But it's crazy!" Frode screamed, rising to his feet and pounding on the table. "Why would I hit my own guys? Why blow up my town? Cops all over the fucking place. A sub-chief of the federal judicial police from Rome on my doorstep while I'm at breakfast."

"I remind you that is why we are here," said Ricercato from Palermo. "You can't keep your Family in line." He shot a quick look at Astio. "Maybe it's time for a change."

"No!"

Into the silence following Frode's terrified shout, Astio said, "As a matter of fact, gentlemen, if I am permitted to speak?"

"Speak!" commanded ice-throated Brinato.

"There is a witness."

They all stared at Don Tronfio.

In a single smoothly gliding move, Astio got from his chair, crossed the room and opened the door. He motioned and a soldier dressed in an obvious imitation of Astio came into the room with Hilde. Astio took the girl's hand and nodded. The soldier withdrew, closing the door. Astio guided the blonde across the deep carpeting and sat her down in the chair he'd just vacated.

"Now, Hilde, tell these gentlemen exactly what you told me. Go on, don't be afraid." A thin edge of raw intimidation came into Astio's voice. "Tell them, exactly."

"I . . . was . . . was with Signor Mezzano—" She swallowed heavily and looked up at Astio standing by her side. Astio put a hand on her shoulder, and she remembered the cruel little Corsican and the incredible pain, and the more recent dose of pain almost as bad, and she flinched under Astio's touch. "Tell them, Hilde."

It all came out in a rush then.

She had been with Mezzano the night before when a man walked in on them.

Yes, she had seen him before. No, not his name, only that others called him Dito, The Finger. He was dressed in black and armed with a long-barreled gun, she did not know what kind. Dito threw one of those, she gestured toward the metal objects on the table, on the bed, and then he laughed. He said the old man was tired of Mezzano skimming off too much from the top of the business for himself.

"And then he just shot him," Hilde said woodenly.

"LIES, LIES, ALLLLL LIES!" Frode cried out, sobbing,

94

beating his fists on the table. He thrust his hand at Astio. "He's taking me down, using Bolan's hits to take me down. Look at that goddam German whore, look *at her!* She's terrified. Strip her, for the sake of God, and you'll find she's been tortured."

Frode leaned across the table. "Tell them, girl. TELL THEM."

Astio's hand squeezed Hilde's shoulder and she shuddered with fear. Astio shouted, "Rana!"

The door opened and the same soldier came into the room. His face had a froglike look, and his imitation of Astio's wardrobe helped his appearance very little. He carried a sack in his left hand.

Astio gestured and Rana came to the table, opened the sack, pulled the bottom corners, and a head rolled out. Even the dons gasped and recoiled with horror and disgust. Hilde screamed and Astio jerked her from the chair by her long blonde hair. He slapped her three times, hard, and she grew silent except for deep, shuddering sobs. Astio pointed.

"Is that the man who killed Mezzano?"

Hilde nodded.

Astio slapped her again. "Look at the face."

He twisted her hair and forced her neck to turn and made her look. "Is that THE MAN?"

"Yes, yes, yes, yes," Hilde screeched and jerked free of Astio's grip, stumbled backwards and fell. At the nod of Astio's head, Rana jerked the girl to her feet and walked her out the door.

"Get rid of that filthy thing," said foppish Ricercato, holding a handkerchief to his face, turning away.

Astio shouted again and Rana returned to the room, rolled the head back into the sack and carried it out.

Astio stood behind his chair and placed his hands on the back. "The head you just saw belonged to Ibrido

Delatore. He has been employed by Don Frode for the past two years, to carry out, ah, special assignments."

After a long pause, Brinato's icy voice broke the silence. "Gentlemen?"

The man from Palermo, leaning back in his chair, said, "I'm ready."

"And I," said Ricercato, wiping his lips.

Brinato looked around the table. The men from Salerno and Genoa, Catania, Messina, Venice, and Reggio, and all the others either nodded emphatically or voiced assent.

Brinato looked down the table toward Frode. "Before we vote, do you have anything more to say?"

"Just this," Frode said, feeling slack and dry and old, and already dead. "Remember what I tell you here. Remember. Because you will have cause to remember." He looked up at Astio. "You will die within a week, the moment you are found out as the traitor you are."

Astio made an obscene gesture.

Frode found himself able to smile. "Cannibal," he responded to the gesture; then returned his attention to the table.

"Remember that Cafu of Agrigento was—not—here! Unlike you, he is home watching his business, fortifying against Bolan. He *knows* Bolan took down my city, and he knows why, as do I. Diversion."

In the sudden silence, the dons stirred restlessly in their chairs. "Of all you, only Don Cafu was not fooled and did not answer the summons for my table."

Frode knew he had not long to live, perhaps five minutes, possibly an hour. He enjoyed watching them become uncertain, sweat, look at one another.

Astio saw it too, and felt his victory slipping away. He spoke fast. "Then why haven't we any reports from elsewhere that Bolan's hit again?"

All the dons nodded and muttered, getting the assurance they needed.

Frode said, "You are so stupid, all of you. Cafu knows. That is why he is not here." He looked around the table. "Do you know why Bolan took Philly and our Angeletti Family down? Because Don Cafu has started a new business. Training soldiers. Mercenary assassins. He rents them to others in this thing of *yours*—not ours, because I know how the vote will go. He rents his soldiers for one thousand U.S. dollars a day, and Bolan took down seventy-five of them in Philly."

Frode paused, then shouted, "NOW VOTE, YOU SONS OF BITCHES!" He abruptly dropped his voice to almost a whisper. "And cut your own motherfucking throats."

He got up and walked out.

An hour later he was dead and lying in a box while Frog poured wet cement over the body.

Only one man at the table knew Frode had told the truth, the man who'd framed him and then killed him, Astio Traditore, just confirmed as new Boss of Bosses in Napoli. Traditore had every resource at his disposal directed toward one single objective: find and kill Mack Bolan before he reached Agrigento. If he failed, Frode's prediction would become precisely true. The dons would discover Traditore had shucked them into killing one of their own, and what the German girl had undergone would seem like Paradise compared to the tortures Astio would suffer before he found relief in death.

The entire Neapolitan organization turned to with a will, each man knowing that dozens of high-echelon vacancies now existed, and the man who made the best impression on the new don would be at the boss' right hand, a favorite, handed the most lucrative action.

No one worked harder than The Frog, who idolized Astio. And it was Frog who turned up the first thin lead, traced it out from the airport and shortly after three o'clock in the morning stopped outside the "home" of a truck driver named Fretta. Frog stepped over the open-ditch stinking sewer and with a soldier at each side, he took down the front door of Fretta's hovel, kicking it in, gun in hand.

Fretta made no pretense whatever of resisting. He knew who these men were, and when they asked, he told them exactly what they wanted to know: the old truck was a faded blue, it had a crumpled right-front fender, there were noticeable rust spots on the hood. The man? The man was big, over six feet tall, weighing at least 95 kilos, perhaps a hundred. And, yes, my masters, he did indeed have eyes like blue-stained ice. Go? I only know he sent me to buy native clothing for him, a few extra cans of gasoline and a crate of oil. The engine on that old truck needed a complete overhaul, valves and rings most, pumped oil like a furnace, looked like an old-time loco-motive coming, gushing blue smoke. I saw no arms, only a large crate of wood which the big man lashed down on the bed of the truck. Yes, he spoke some Italian, not such fine grammar, Sicilian dialect, looked *Siciliano,* to me. Of course, at your orders, always.

That they let him keep the new truck and did not damage it sent Fretta into such a fit of astonishment he decided to see a priest first thing tomorrow and legalize his marriage to the woman he'd lived with for nineteen years and who had borne all his eleven children.

When the old truck quit on him, finally expiring by suiciding itself when it threw a rod through the block within sight of Reggio, Mack Bolan had no idea how lucky that seemingly disastrous incident was.

Because during the last hours of darkness, Traditore, Frog, and four soldiers had chartered a plane and flown to Reggio. Traditore knew he should have been in Naples consolidating his new position, but at the same time he knew there would be no position, and he would be too dead to fill it, unless he got Mack Bolan, The Executioner, and took him down forever.

Afraid to notify the Reggio don and recruit gunmen because that might expose his cannibalistic testimony which liquidated Don Tronfio, Astio had no choice other than recruiting and arming low-grade freelance local help, some of whom Frog had to show how to load their weapons.

Then Astio spread dollars around, merchants, street hawkers, taxi drivers, shoeshine boys, everyone he could think of who might by remotest possibility spot Bolan coming into town, or see him if he was already in Reggio. Then Astio could only sit back and wait for Bolan to come into the trap, and Bolan did.

11: REGGIO RAGAZZA

Alma Bellezza had finished her morning milking, turned the cattle out, strained the milk through clean white sacking into pails, loaded the pails with sealed lids on the cart, and had the team hitched, when she heard the truck coming.

She looked up as the old blue junker went past, moving hardly as fast as she could walk, rattling, and from its guts coming a fearful clatter. Stinking blue smoke fogged from the exhaust pipe.

Then she noticed the driver. Her loins trembled and her breath caught, and she felt the nipples of her bosoms stiffen. Even as he sat in the cab of the truck, he looked immense; and she quivered under the fleeting gaze and white smile he gave her as he nursed the truck along the poor road toward the city. If she hurried, she could overtake him, perhaps. She started to climb up on the wagon, then changed her mind and ran back into the house. She emerged a few moments later in a fresh dress, her hands and arms and ankles freshly washed, and wearing her best bonnet. She checked the milk cans again, then climbed upon the seat and urged the astonished horses into a brisk trot. Ten minutes later, her heart seemed to come up into her mouth as she topped a rise and saw at the bottom of the hill that the truck had pulled off to one side, and the man was out with his head stuck down inside the engine box.

She slowed the horses.

Bolan had caught the movement on the road at the top of the hill when the team came into sight. He did not turn his head but a fraction of an inch, so he could see from the side of his eye, and recognized the milk-maid from the farm he'd just passed. He noticed at once that she had changed clothes. Eyes narrowed against the searing Calabrian glare, Mack unkinked his back and turned to face the approaching wagon. He saw she had gone to more than ordinary trouble, so—maybe . . . just maybe.

He did not step into the road in an effort to stop the horses, but only moved a couple of steps, removed his cap politely and said, *"Buon giorno, signorina."*

With trembling hands and a flutter in her breast, Alma pulled the team to a halt. *"Buon giorno."*

She could not trust herself to say more. Her throat choked, and her chin felt unsteady. Never in her life had she seen such a man, not even in the cinema. Except, perhaps, Raf Vallone? No, not even he.

The man gestured toward the truck. *"Ma la mia baratto ha un guasto."*

Broken down, I should think so! Alma thought. A miracle he came so far. What a peculiar accent he had. Was it Sicilian? He also spoke with his eyes. She said, *"È possibile rimorchiarla?"*

Bolan shrugged with what he hoped was authentic Latin eloquence. He thought the girl asked if it were possible to tow the truck. He couldn't hack it that well, so he returned to his deaf-mute act, modified version, as though he had a serious and humiliating speech impediment. The comely girl's instant sympathy made him feel almost ashamed. With gestures and guttural words, he made her understand the possibility of transferring his crate from the truck to her wagon. Once she understood, Alma expertly handled the team, backing the wagon, then pulling alongside the truckbed, tying the lines, climbing up and with a strength that astonished Bolan, helped him lift the heavy crate up and slide it off the truck onto the wagon.

Bolan shook his head in wonderment, smiling, mumbled, *"Grazie,"* and flexed his bicep, then touched her upper arm. *"Potente!"* he said, indicating her strength. Alma blushed so hard she felt as though she might go up in a sheet of flame. And her knees felt weak as smoke when the vast blue-eyed man took her arm gently and turned her, jumped to the ground and pulled her so she fell off the wagon into his arms, feeling her strong heavy breasts against him. For a moment he held her, then in three long effortless strides carried her to the seat and placed her upon it as though she were a child and not a one-hundred-forty-pound farm girl whose usual day began with milking seven cows, forking feed to them, carrying water to the house, plowing, cultivating, harvesting as the seasons came and went, trapping her endlessly in a poverty of bare existence. More than once she had lain awake at night and thought of leaving, even if she fell into the life nearly all girls of her class did when they went to the cities. She did not believe she would mind the men so much, that was only a natural thing, making love; but Alma had heard too many stories about the other things, the drugs and cruelty and unbelievable demands often made upon prostitutes; and she knew she could never stand all that, and spending her last final

103

days as a diseased, wrinkled, useless commodity performing unspeakable acts with animals before drunken sailors in Tangiers, Marseille, or Port Said.

She wondered what was in the crate. *Dio,* how heavy! Alma watched the beautiful man get an old pasteboard suitcase from the cab of the truck, and then with the lithe grace of a panther, climb up beside her on the seat, smiling. She unwound the reins and clucked the horses into motion, wondering why the man did not remove his old shapeless coat; it was such a fine warm morning.

Bolan saw the first pair of them waiting for him from almost a half-mile away. Local toughs Astio had hired. My thinking was right, anyway, Bolan thought. Astio called the dons' table on his one-time boss, and took him down. But Astio had moved *fast!* Bolan knew the truck driver had dropped his mud. Probably they hadn't even questioned Teaf. In fact, the pilot probably had gotten his ass out of Naples and on the way home in one hell of a hurry. A creep and totally greedy asshole Teaf was, but stupid he'd proved himself not.

The Reggio local freelancers gave themselves away by their actions. They displayed themselves by imitating hardguys. Look at me, Ma. Got a gun. Showing off in front of the babes.

Bolan felt sure that if they recognized him, they had orders not to shoot. Astio would want Bolan for himself, and Astio would engineer a way to get Bolan's head in a sack and collect the bounty money, too. Putting it all together damned nicely.

Humped over as though ill, cap pulled low across his eyes, Alma driving the team at a slow, regular, unconcerned pace, Bolan passed the outer guards unnoticed.

But as Alma drove deeper into the city, wending through the narrow streets, Bolan noticed the close attention every person with possible Mafia connections paid to all traffic. Taxi-drivers ignored fares for closer looks at old trucks, waiters stood in the doorways of cafes, bartenders looked out windows, and twice, then three times Bolan saw the gazes of men inspect him, travel on, them come back for another, closer look.

Bolan knew it was the coat. Everyone else in shirtsleeves, the day growing hotter by the moment. The coat was the kind of thing cops and criminals alike automatically watched for—something out of the ordinary. Like a skinny, hinky dude skating along the bricks with sweat pouring off him while he wore a long-sleeved shirt with the cuffs buttoned. To hide the needle tracks from heroin injections on the veins inside his elbows. Bolan had to get out of the coat.

He crawled over the back of the wagon seat and dropped down between it and his crate, unholstered the Beretta and put his cap over it, shucked out of the coat and stripped off the shoulder rig, rolled it and stuffed it into one coat pocket, got the Beretta in his right hand, slapped his cap back on. Holding the pistol with the coat draped over it, he climbed back up beside Alma, smiling reassurance.

Again with gestures and a few words, Bolan got it across to Alma that he wished to buy her lunch and also pay her for helping him. He also needed a place to unload his crate and rest for a while. The last suggestion brought a fresh-blooming blush to her round tanned cheeks and feeling like a bastard because he was using her, Bolan put his arm around the girl and hugged her tightly, big hand sliding up under her arm along the rich firm curve of her bosom. He nuzzled her neck until she giggled and pulled away, talking fast. He had no idea what she said, except, *Wait, wait!*

She drove to the creamery and Bolan helped her unload the milk, then stood by and watched in amusement and some astonishment as Alma turned from the shy, ripe, virginal milkmaid into a tough and experienced haggler with a raucous machinegunning voice, and finally she evidently got her price because the dockboss suddenly threw up his hands as though giving his heart, soul and wife and children and every *lira* he owned to a perfect stranger, probably Satan in disguise. After a moment, he returned from his office and carefully counted out the money. Alma counted it again, then shoved it down between her breasts while the dockboss leered. She sniffed at him, then emptied her milk cans into a large vat, rinsed the cans clean under a nearby faucet, then put the empties back on the wagon.

The odors of manure and ammonia rose so strongly from the stableyard, Bolan seemed to be lying in a tub filled with them. But of the three places Alma showed him, Bolan chose this one because it afforded him the best protection against sudden attack, and the best observation post.

He had a wide open view down the sloping street toward the dock where the ferry tied up. His back was protected by another building jammed against the stable and hayloft. Alma's horses had rolled in the thick dust, drank from the water trough, and now munched thin feed in the shade.

Bolan heard a sigh behind him and turned from the window. He felt more like a bastard than ever when he looked at the girl. Despite her extremely well-developed body, she could not be more than twenty. When he took her he'd felt like a ruthless cradle-robber, except that he'd been taken as much as he took. And though he discovered this had not been her first time, it was hardly more than the second or third, she was so trembly and awkward, yet frantically eager. She sighed again in her sleep, totally satiated. Bolan returned to his watch.

So far he had spotted six of them, four local, cheap

gunsels, who like the others watching the road into town, spent most of their time imitating themselves. The other two, though, were real hardguys. While the gunsels strutted and preened, the hardmen prowled unobtrusively, or took up posts along the most likely approaches and rested in the shade, conserving themselves.

And then each time the ferry came across the Strait of Messina, only two miles wide at its narrowest, from Messina to Reggio, Bolan watched a dozen more hardmen and that many or more gunsels working through the crowd gathered to catch the ferry.

Upon each docking, Bolan watched carefully; and the routine never varied. Not one of the gunmen ever gave a single glance toward the incoming vessel, nor paid any attention to the disembarking passengers.

Now Bolan had his battle ops worked out. He went to the bed, lay down beside Alma, not awakening her, set his never-fail mental alarm, and slept until evening. When he woke, Alma sat on a stool beside a large crockery basin, bathing herself with a cloth. She smiled whitely as Bolan sat up, turned more to face him, naked and gleaming. Bolan grinned at her, and she rose and came to him.

Afterwards, Bolan told her what he wanted her to do. He dropped the pose and used all the Italian at his command, considerable since he'd dealt so intimately with Mafia types for so long. He saw that the change in him frightened her, but she was so thoroughly taken with him, she questioned nothing he said.

She got dressed and went out. Bolan went down to the crate, opened it, and in the gloom of the stable's back stalls, he dressed in his black combat garb. He wrapped the Beretta and .44 Automag in waterproofing, as well as extra ammo clips. He started to take along two frags, then put them back. The dockside became thickly crowded and all a grenade would do was take down innocents.

Mack slipped his peasant disguise back on, closed the crate, went out and met Alma as she returned. He helped her harness the team to the wagon, then took the paint can and brush she had bought and climbed up into the wagon. He addressed the crate to himself, MAGO BOEMO, The Bohemian Magician, *will call,* at the office of a freight company Alma told him had offices in Catania. For a moment, Bolan wryly considered addressing the crate to himself as *Il Boia*: *The Executioner.* But he had survived so far in his war against the Mafia because he refused to underestimate his enemy, no matter how many of them had fallen under his guns and grenades, his blitzing attacks across the U.S. and parts of Europe.

While Alma went inside to pay the stableman, Bolan opened one of the milk cans and dropped a thousand dollars in Mafia money down into the can, then sealed it tightly. When she returned, he made her go through the instructions again.

She was to haul the crate to the dock, pre-pay its passage to Messina on the ferry, then by truck to Catania. She was to sling in an appropriate *puntale* or *"bustarella"*—tip, bribe, to insure the magician's box got preferential treatment.

Alma returned thirty minutes later with the manifest, and Bolan lied to her: "I have to see some men in the city. I'll be back before eleven." He took her elbows and held them tightly. "Listen to me. Listen exactly. Whatever you do, stay–away–from–the–truck. Understand? *Do not touch the truck.*"

Bolan knew that by this time Astio had sent scouts up the roads leading from Reggio, and by now they had found and booby-trapped the truck. He wished he had time to go back to it and blow it up himself. One hit from the .44 Automag would jar off the detonators.

But maybe not. When they saw the crate gone . . . and surely the truckdriver, Fretta, had told Astio about the crate . . . they would not plant the truck, maybe. Bolan hoped to Christ not.

Bolan kissed her one last time, and then before Alma knew or even saw, the big man vanished into the evening gloom. She felt wet on her face, and realized she was crying. She knew he would never be back, when she thought about his return at eleven. Wearily, with a sorrow that stuck in her throat and felt like a knife in her guts, she climbed upon the wagon seat and slapped the lines across the horses' rumps. She could be home well before eleven, and he was never coming back, and the cows were by now standing at the waterlot gate, bawling with thirst and hunger and swollen udders. She wondered who he was, and shifted her weight on the rough seat as something seemed to stick her in the thigh. She felt and found a metal object in the pocket of her apron and took it out. It was a cross unlike any she had ever seen before. She looked at it until her vision blurred with tears, then she wiped her eyes, kissed the cross and dropped it between her breasts, where she would wear it forever.

She had driven to within sight of the last street lights on the road out of Reggio when they took her.

A man came from each side of the road, out of the shadows, and in the same instant, two climbed over the endgate; all had guns. One, who looked like a frog, laid his gunbarrel upside her jaw and in reflex action she slammed him in the face with her fist, putting her shoulder and all hundred-forty pounds of work-hardened farm girl behind the punch. Frog went off backwards and landed on his head in the street, convulsively clenching his hands, and shooting the left horse of Alma's team through the heart. The horse lunged, sprayed blood through both nostrils, then dropped in his tracks. The other horse spooked, lunging and kicking, almost upsetting the wagon.

One of the gunsels lost his head and clubbed Alma

109

across the top of her skull with his pistol, just as Ragno shouted, "No!" But it was too late.

Alma went slack as a dead and toppled out of the wagon.

Ragmo caught her, but her weight bore his gangly frame to the ground. A car pulled from a narrow street and two men jumped out, grabbed Alma and threw her inside. Ragno, The Spider, rose shakily to his feet and climbed in behind them. The driver knelt beside Rana, feeling his pulse. He shrugged and picked up The Frog's gun, and started back to the car. The gunsel, still on the wagon seat, shouted, "Hey, what about me? I got her. I got pay coming."

From the car a voice issued a command.

The driver turned and aimed with Frog's gun and shot the gunsel through the head. "Paid in full, stupid."

In the car, pulling away, the wheelman asked, "She dead?"

"No, damned lucky for us. Astio'd have our balls roasting over a slow fire."

"She broke Frog's neck, knocking him off right on top of his head."

"You sure she's the one?"

"Who helped Bolan? Who the hell knows? She *is* the one the boss said watch for. From that farm just beyond where he left the truck."

"Okay, hook it up. The boss is getting antsy as hell."

The wheelman drove toward the dock.

12: REGGIO REPULISTI

Bolan went into the water a mile and a half above the ferry dock, swimming easily in the warm waters of the Strait. His clothing and the weight of the weapons and extra ammo hindered him, but he'd given himself plenty of time and swam without tiring himself.

The ferry was still hull down on the horizon of the sea when he entered the water, only its truck light showing, but as he swam, the running lights came into view, then the lighted deck, and Bolan began easing in toward the ferry's course. He was almost a mile offshore when he turned and added power to his even strokes and came across the bow, treaded water and let the boat pass, then fell in its wake, pouring it on. The same line he had observed three times earlier in the day still trailed carelessly in the water off the port stern, and Bolan caught it. He worked his way up the rope, hand over hand against the force of the boat pulling him through the water, wrapped his right leg around the trailing slack, drew the

111

leg up and caught the slack, and in a moment had a bowline-on-bight in the line. Mack slipped his right foot into the non-slip loop, passed the line under his right arm, across his back, under his left arm, and in a sort of cradle, he rode along buffeting in the foaming wake.

When the ferry slowed, Mack instantly used his right hand as a rudder and swung his body out to the side and looked past the ferry. The Reggio landing was less than two hundred yards away.

Bolan went hand over hand, fast, up the rope to the side of the ferryboat, placed his feet against the slippery sea-slick hull, and climbed. As he knew they would—it was only natural—everyone aboard faced the dock and the city. What was there to see back across the Strait? In a moment, he was aboard.

Thanks to his *ragazza*, his girl Alma from Reggio, Bolan was on the ferry to Sicily, and in a few minutes his warchest, the Bohemian Magician's crate, would also be aboard. A mile or so out of Messina on the crossing, he would drop over the side and swim ashore, then cut inland to the Messina-Catania road, flag a bus or wagon, or hire a taxi, hole up in Catania until his warchest arrived, then across the island along the base of snow-capped Mount Etna, to Enna, then the road southwest from the junction at Caltanissetta, through Canicatti and Naro, and then—

Then he would have to see. Another long-range penetration behind enemy lines. He would be in Indian country at Naro, Agrigento Province, and somewhere back in the convulsively upthrust mountainous and canyon-slashed boondocks, he would find Don Cafu's *Scuola Assassino,* School for Assassins.

It was becoming so ridiculously easy, Mack Bolan felt the hair on his neck bristle in warning. It had become *too* easy.

He was a known and hunted man in a foreign country

on a mission of death and destruction, and since leaving Naples airport it had all gone his way, virtually without a hitch. Bolan was good and knew he was good and he'd survived because he was better than good, because he was The Executioner, man with a mission, and incomprehensibly efficient, to the Mafia's bitter knowledge and experience. He was so good that more than once the "membership" had sent the word out: come and reason with us, join us.

When you can't beat 'em, join 'em. . . .

Bolan knew he'd have lasted inside the Mafia about as long as a crooked cop in the regular jail lockup. Until he was exhausted and had fought as long as he could. Then they would make pulp of his head with their heels.

For the cons in the tank, the cop had to go just on general principles.

Inside the Mafia, identified, Bolan had to go because no man, no organization, including the United States Government—and all its enforcement agencies, FBI, Bureau of Narcotics, Customs, Alcohol & Tobacco Tax Unit, and the Department of Justice Organized Crime Task Force—none of them, nor all of them combined, had taken down as many *mafioso* as this one single man, Mack Bolan, The Executioner.

The bastard Bolan was an earthquake, a timebomb, an off-duty cop, a drunk driver bent upon suicide all in one package—totally unpredictable and no way, no–fucking –WAY! To get handles on the guy. To figure him. His next move. Christ, how do you make plans for a bastard who goes through San Diego like water through a hose and a couple of days later wipes out Frank Angeletti's soldier barracks in Philadelphia? Then shows up *inside* Don Stefano's home impersonating Wild Card Cavaretta so well the son of a bitch sleeps, actually *sleeps* in the don's house, before taking the whole fucking place down!

Perhaps the "members" could have understood better if one of them had ever had a look at Mack Bolan's journals!

I'm already dead. In old Norse mythology, so I understand, there is a place called Valhalla. All the great warriors gather there nightly to dine and drink and be entertained, and then fight to the death. Guts ripped out, heads lopped off, blinded and maimed— And yet the next night, they return whole and well, to dine and drink and fight again.

They are dead but don't know it.

Am I in my own personal Valhalla . . . ?

It doesn't matter. I will keep on fighting until I can fight no more, the way I have always fought, and for the same reasons. The Law cannot do the job, hamstrung and handcuffed by red tape, rules, regulations, books, court decisions. I am not and will never be. So long as I last, I will continue the fight.

Bolan found the portside aft head, stepped inside and stripped off after locking the door. He wrung out his outer clothing, checked his weapons and ammo and found them safely dry, dressed again, then came out on deck as the ferry slowed and began swinging around, stern toward the dock, using the Mediterranean moor, a device the U.S. Navy had made so popular. When ships tied-to with their sterns to the dock, they could get underway in seconds, without delicate dockside maneuvering or using tugs to come alongside or depart. The "Med moor" also saved a hell of a lot of docking space, quayside.

As the ferry swung around, stern toward dock, Bolan moved toward the bow. He let his narrowed gaze rove over the crowd, picking out the *mafiosi* and the gunsels

114

he'd spotted earlier in the day. He spotted the gunsels as easily as before. A gun gave some types of guys a lot of balls. He felt his hackles bristle again. Where was Rana, the frog-faced dude? He'd been obviously in charge of the dockcrew, all during the day while Bolan watched from the hayloft room. Now he was gone.

Then Bolan saw them.

Alma had a huge jawbust lump on the left side of her face, and a glob of red showed on the top of her bonnet. On her left stood a gangly spiderlike man with his hand in his right pocket, bulging. On her right stood Astio, and Bolan saw his lips moving.

Alma shook her head.

As though there were no one, much less the more than a hundred people on the dock, disembarking and waiting to board the ferry, Astio turned and almost casually drove his right fist into Alma's face and broke her nose. Blood sprayed, and Bolan saw her buckle at the knees under the force of the deliberately smashing punch. Then she shook her head, raised her chin, and spat a mouthful of blood into Astio's face.

Somehow, someway, Mack Bolan vowed to himself, he would make it up to that girl. He would find a way, by God. Alma, it meant *soul;* and she had it, from the core out.

First, though, he had to save her life. Astio would never stand for that spitting in his face.

Almost reluctantly, Mack pulled the Beretta, checked that the silencer was screwed firmly in place, rested his elbows on an engine-room blower stack, sighted, and shot Astio Traditore through the head. He swung a fraction to his right and shot Spider between the eyes.

Immediately, the wheelman leaped from the car, gun drawn, staring around. He moved around the front of the car and Bolan shot him through the throat.

Without discipline, eager only for heroics and a big

115

payday, the gunsels came to Astio's "rescue." Then stood in a muttering gang, looking about, seeking a target.

The people of Reggio paid them no attention. Since time began, the old stories and even the Bible itself told of such happenings in the streets of Reggio, Rome, Bethlehem, along the ancient Appian Way.

There were people in the crowd who would have traded places with the deads, despite their abject suffering poverty.

The priests had warned them that pain and torture and suffering beyond imagination awaited those who suicided themselves. So the people of Reggio plodded onwards, unseeing. That men had achieved a walk on the moon meant absolutely nothing to them. Most of them did not know. Of those who knew, nearly all did not believe. Blood running in the streets was Reggio. Was Calabria. Italy. They walked on past, looking neither right or left, minds purposely blank.

The dockworkers, too, accustomed to oppression by Mafia labor bosses, knowing the less seen and heard the better, simply went about their work as though three dead men and the gunwaving gunsels did not exist. Mack watched, and saw the *bustarella,* the little bribe, tip, had worked. Bolan's crated warchest was first aboard.

Then it was time to break it up and let Alma out. The cheap gunsels had started some big behavior. In a ludicrous imitation of the real merchandise, one gunsel twisted up a handful of Alma's hair and jerked her head back so the cords in her neck stood out like cables and her outsized bosom seemed ready to burst through her dress.

Bolan saw the longshoremen return to dockside after loading his crate. He holstered the Beretta and drew the .44 Automag. He shot the gunsel holding Alma. The big, high-impact slug went in just under the gunsel's chin, hit with crushingly expanding force, and tore the man's head

116

from his body. It rolled down the slight incline toward the dock, and became lost among the shuffling feet of the people who refused to look, refused to acknowledge they walked between the front lines of a war between two opposing forces.

Bolan fired again, twice more, shooting lower now, taking the guts out of the cheap thugs who'd come ganging around Alma. He wanted them to have a look at what it was all about, this hiring out cheap, packing heat, strutting before the girls, bragging it up. Bolan wanted their brothers and sisters and all their relatives to see what it cost. Working a dirt farm in Calabria wasn't much of a life, and grubbing for coins along the waterfront little better; but they did not get you dead like mixing with "that thing of theirs" did. It didn't get your bloody yellow guts slopped out on the quay with a hole the size of a football in your back where the .44 Magnum emerged, spraying bone splinters, sticky wet red, slimy yellow.

Bolan got them all, a *cleansweep*. A Reggio Repulisti!

In Messina, in Catania, and for damned sure in Agrigento the "membership" awaited him, Bolan knew. But right now he was on the way . . . to the Mafia's homeground, its birthplace. Sicily. Because he went into the wheelhouse and told the captain, "Get underway."

The captain shouted just three words, slowly, so there would be no misunderstanding. "Cut all lines."

He looked at Bolan, and The Executioner nodded. With the "Med moor" all the captain had to do was call the engine room and order, "All ahead flank."

It was like putting a car in passing gear. Going past full-speed-ahead, asking for maximum revs the engines could make.

Mack picked up the captain's binoculars and looked back at dockside. He saw brave Alma standing among the littered deads, waving. Bolan owed that girl plenty, and somehow he would see she got paid. He knew that by now if the "members" or the gunsels had not looted her milkcan, the street punks of Reggio had. He vowed to square it with her.

In the meantime, thanks to his *ragazza*, his girl Alma, he'd made a cleansweep: *Reggio Repulisti!*

13: CROSSING & BEACHHEAD

No more than fifty passengers had managed to board the ferry before Bolan ordered the lines cut and all-ahead flank. There was one policeman aboard, an "airplane" as the *carabinieri* were called because of their hats, which looked like slick shellacked sailplanes about ready to lift into flight on the outspread wings. Bolan had determined that the captain of the ferry spoke passable English, the kind of English many fishermen working boats out of San Francisco, California spoke.

That was to say, he understood every word, and the inflection Bolan placed upon every word; but he did not speak good English because he was ashamed of his accent.

At Bolan's command, the captain called the airplane to the wheel house. When the carabinieri stepped into the cramped quarters, still quite neat and stylish despite his ordeal, Bolan put the cold wet muzzle of the .44 Automag in the airplane's ear. The man stiffened and raised his hands high above his head, and Bolan disarmed him of his submachinegun and belt pistol.

Bolan asked the captain. "You have a raft?"

"Certainly."

"Are these waters dangerous this time of year."

"Not at all."

"Have a man break out a raft. Supply it well with water and some food. Drop it over the side on a tow line. Put this airplane into the raft safely, then proceed."

Bolan smiled nonchalantly. "I'll kill the first man moves wrong. You first, Captain."

"Not worry!"

Three minutes later a furious, disarmed *carabinieri* wearing nothing but his underwear and his hat floated alone in the darkness of the Strait of Messina. In an enraged fury of anger, the policeman ripped off his hat and threw it with all his strength. To his amazement, the hat flew like a goddam airplane! All his career he'd resented the whispered defamatory term, "airplane," and now in the moon and starlight he found it true.

The goddam hat skimmed out across the dark water, caught an updraft, spun round and round, rose to a hundred, then perhaps a hundred-and-thirty feet, sailed, and finally vanished from the policeman's sight in the darkness. The only thing he could see was the diminishing lights of the ferryboat. With the magnificent Latin philosophical attitude, knowing he could do nothing whatever about the ferry and the huge man who'd taken command, the airplane got to his feet, steadied himself, and peed over the side.

Finished with his business, he lit a cigarette and made himself comfortable. It was a long time till daylight.

Mack Bolan wished for a night fifteen hours long, instead of one so short as this night in late spring so near the equator. He spoke to the captain. "How long for the crossing?"

The captain shrugged, with the kind of Latin eloquence Bolan tried earlier to imitate, not especially successfully.

"It depends, signor, upon the wind, the seas, the tide."

Bolan showed the captain the Beretta.

"There are no tides in the Mediterranean."

"Ah, so, yes. But in the Strait, she is different. Huh? Meeting our Tyrian Sea with the Med."

"Old man," Bolan said flatly, ruthlessly, without remorse, "I can see the island now. Sicily. The big vast dark shape rising out of the sea." Bolan paused, and laid the icy cold iron along the side of the shipmaster's face. "There is no way I can miss it. Agreed?"

"Si, signor."

"Surely you have no stupid idea of dying on my account. I've harmed no crewman, set the airplane free, have not even inquired about your safe, correct?"

"Assolutamente, signor! Absolutely, sir!"

"You have valuables in the safe?"

The captain hesitated just a fraction of a second too long, so when he answered, Bolan knew the captain lied. "No, no valuables."

"You lied. But no matter. Take them for yourself and blame it on me." Bolan laughed coarsely. "What else, eh?"

The captain did not reply.

"Now, you are on course, correct?" Bolan asked. Then sarcastically—"Allowing for the tide and winds and so forth, naturally."

"I am on course."

"Stay so and you have nothing—listen to me! Nothing to worry about, understand?"

"Si, signor."

"I am leaving the wheelhouse now, scouting around;

121

but you saw the devastation of this gun I hold. Now, you son of a bitch are you going to maintain course for Messina or what?"

"Straight on course, absolutely."

"Or the ship has a new captain."

And before the ship's master was sure the black-clad big man was gone, he was alone.

Bolan slithered across hatches and found the aft hold. He lifted the cover and squirmed down inside. With a penlight he located his crate. Sweating and struggling, he shifted the cargo so the crate would be first unloaded, then he went back topside. The lights of Messina had come into view.

Bolan found his peasant clothing, rolled it into a bundle and covered it with a large plastic bag, moved to the port railing, drew the .44 Automag and sent a thundering shot through the wheelhouse, deliberately wide, missing the captain, but sending along the message.

Then he rewrapped the Automag in protective covering and secured it and fell off the port rail, landing on his back. Twenty minutes later Bolan was ashore. In the brittle starlight and late cast of the dying moon, he could look almost straight up and see the snow-capped towering loom of Mount Etna.

He found a hidden cavelike cove amongst the rocks, dragged in driftwood and built a fire. He stripped off his skintight black combat garb, removed the ammo, maps, emergency rations and other equipment, and stood before the fire to warm. He checked his watch. Plenty of time. He broke open a kit of rations, ate the concentrated vitamin/high-protein bars, then allowed himself the luxury of a single cup of coffee while he smoked a cigarette.

Then he lay on the sand with his feet to the fire, set his mental never-fail alarm, and slept until an hour before dawn. In six minutes Bolan was up and moving, having erased every trace of his landing, of his existence. As the blood-red rising sun rose upward across the eastern horizon, Bolan squatted in hiding beside the Messina-Catania road, wearing the rough, ill-fitting, unpressed peasant costume over his weapons and black combat suit.

There was hardly any traffic. Bolan had to accustom himself to that. As he'd done in Calabria. Christ, back in the states in Metropolitan New England/New York/D.C. —all along the Atlantic Seaboard between Boston and Virginia, it was a lousy 24-hour-a-day scramble. He'd seen people who couldn't afford a $7 taxi fare to Manhattan wait two and a half hours in a stone blizzard at La Guardia for a bus: fare, two bucks.

On the other hand, it simplified Bolan's problem.

He knew the name of the freighter. He had the manifest wrapped in oilskin in his pocket. He had chosen the crest of a long grinding grade for his watchpoint. Bolan chuckled to himself, remembering when he'd done his research on Sicily. Some professor writing for one of the encyclopedias dismissed the Mafia with a single sentence:

> *"The Mafia as such, and organized brigandage, no longer exist on the island."*

Bolan had a lunch of cheese and wine. He did not smoke. He waited. At two in the afternoon he drank another slug of the wine. He waited. During the whole day nine cars and eleven trucks passed.

Shortly before sundown he saw a truck coming that bore both the name and the colors of the hauler who was supposed to have The Bohemian Magician's gear aboard.

Bolan crept out of hiding, staying concealed by roadside vegetation, caught the tailgate of the truck as it passed. He climbed inside, knife ready, slashed the ropes and quilted coverings . . . and found nothing.

123

He eased back and dropped off the truck, returned to his hiding place and waited, wondering. Would the cartage company send a night truck?

There was not that much business on Sicily.

Bolan felt a little sick.

He felt as though he'd been had.

He felt his neck hair bristle again. Okay, they had him made. No matter who. The cops, the "members." The next truck would have his gear, and a load of empty boxes. Inside each box, if large enough, would crouch a soldier, armed, ready, eager to collect the bounty on Mack Bolan.

Bolan eased back into concealment and checked his map. The plan sprang instantly to the front of his agile mind, but it depended entirely upon his own physical stamina and capability.

At first he felt completely confident. Hell, he could do *anything!* A moment later his combat senses took control and he worked it out.

It was just possible.

Just.

As the gloom of night descended, Bolan stripped to his black commando uniform, darkened his face and hands. And just as twilight settled in, the sun lowering behind the ten-thousand-plus feet of Mount Etna, Bolan heard the truck laboring up the hill toward him.

He let the truck go by, watching the cab. A soldier from Naples, an insignificant punk called Rapa, The Turnip, sat behind the wheel. Alone.

Like hell, Bolan thought, watching. Turnip was crammed against the far door, as though he had six guys out of sight in the cab with him.

Bolan let the truck go past, then fell in behind it at a slow jog, all it took to keep up on the steep grade. He flashed his penlight on the freight. One case, his own with the MAGO marking, showed evidence of being solidly nailed down. Five other large wooden boxes. . . .

With a fingernail a man could lift the lids!

Okay, figure a minimum of two hardmen to the box. That made ten. The Beretta held eight 9mm Parabellums in a pistol-grip magazine, and one round chambered, a total of nine shots. Nine deadly crunchers. *Phutting* death. With the silencer, the Beretta made the sound of a smothered cough.

Still, ten men . . . nine shots. That was with a full magazine of eight and a round chambered. A man left over. An armed man.

All right. Then four shots each in the first two boxes. Change clips, three each in the remaining three boxes.

Then you are empty, Bolan told himself.

I am empty of silenced pistol shots. I still have a huge, bucking, silvered .44 Automag. I will not be exactly defenseless.

Bolan jogged along behind the truck as it slowed to a crawl near the top of the high ridge, then started down the other side, gaining speed rapidly, bouncing and swaying and when the rear wheels hit an unpaved rough spot, Bolan swung aboard. He kept low on his belly. Rapa, the driver, had either been given instructions or figured for himself he wanted the rearview mirror operable, giving him a view out through the covered back of the truck.

Bolan kept to the left and crawled forward. When he reached the first box, he rapped on it with his knuckle and muttered.

The box moved squeaking, and Bolan rapped again. The lid suddenly popped open and two men stood up. Bolan shot them both between the eyes, one, one, and let them collapse back into the box. He squirmed around, got his back braced against his own heavy MAGO crate, placed his feet against the other and shoved.

The box containing the two deads went off the tailgate

and shattered, dumping the two limp bodies across the road.

Bolan simplified matters for himself and reloaded his Beretta clip. Then he rose to his feet, leaned a hip against the side of the swaying truck, drew the .44 Automag with his right hand after taking the Beretta in his left, and shot all the packing cases besides his own full of holes.

At the first crashing report of the .44 Automag, the truck swayed violently, walked back and forth across the crude highway, nearing the precipice on one side, the high cliff wall on the other.

In swift succession, while the driver still whipped from side to side in panic, Bolan shoved and pushed the other crates and toppled them end over end, and sent them off the tailgate, shattering to kindling, leaving bodies strewn.

Bolan punched the magazine release buttons on both weapons and reloaded.

Sidling up to the back window, Bolan looked into the cab.

Besides Turnip, two other armed men crouched in the floor board. Bolan shot them both in the top of the head, one, two. And through the shattered window shouted, "Pull up!"

Turnip switched off the key and with trembling hands guided the truck to a stop. Turnip proved himself not only a man with a ridiculously descriptive nickname and a fair truckdriver but also a fool. He went for the gun inside his shirt and Bolan blew the front of Rapa's face off, catapulting him down the steep seaside of the highway.

Bolan climbed into the cab, dragged the other two bodies out and tossed them over the cliffside toward the grumbling surf below. He got in under the wheel, switched on, let the truck roll, slipped into high gear on the downgrade, popped the clutch loose and let the engine catch.

In the light of new day, he filled with gas in Catania and turned west.

Beachhead established and consolidated. Issue no longer in doubt.

14: THE SECOND TABLE

None of the dons cared to look directly at one another. They all knew they'd been had, and each of them felt so helplessly frustrated with anger, none wanted the job of speaking first—of bringing the subject out.

Finally, the Roman, Brinato said, "Well, whadda we gonna do, sit here with our thumbs up our butts all night?"

"The first thing we gotta do," said Vandalo, "is get Naples back under control. I sent some of my boys—"

"*You* sent some of *your* boys?" demanded Ricercato. "And where you get off with that shit? *You* sent *your* boys."

"Somebody had to get in there fast, and the rest of you—" Vandalo gestured obscenely. "Sitting around on your asses while the whole organization falls apart."

"*Shut up!*" Brinato roared in his gravelly voice. "Knock it to hell *off!*" He glared around the room. "This is just what Bolan wants, us squabbling, fighting amongst

129

ourselves, going to war over Naples." Brinato shot looks of anger at each don around the table; they looked back at him, and shifted uneasily in their chairs. "I say for right now, Naples is open. We got a lot bigger worry on our backs than Naples . . . that goddam Bolan!"

Brinato stared at them again. "Now, anybody argue with that?"

No one answered.

"Okay! Now, you, Ruvido," Brinato demanded of the man from Reggio, "what did you find out from that *ragazza,* that girl Alma, right?"

"Nothing. A dumbass farmer. She didn't even know who she was helping, his name or nothing. She was so dumb she still carried one of them marksman medals in her blouse, didn't know any better."

"But you took the farm apart, just to make sure Bolan didn't double back."

"What the hell you take me for?" Ruvido said, insulted.

"Okay, okay, save the ruffled feathers for later."

"He's on the island," Ricercato said, primly.

"And passed right through your fucking town," snapped Vandalo. "Drove right into Catania and filled up with gas and ate breakfast in plain sight, and then . . . *phutt!* Vanished."

"Tell *me* about it!" snapped Paffuto, the chubby boss of Messina. "Those were *my* soldiers he blew up, *my* truck he stole. That *bastard.*" Paffuto's fat hands worked as though he held Bolan's throat in them.

"Let's just cut the crap," Brinato said flatly. "Stop whining about who lost what, and who made this mistake or that fuckup. Okay, goddammit? You guys ready to talk now? You ready to make some *plans,* use your heads, THINK!" In a rage, Brinato shoved back from the table so hard his heavy chair upset and clattered halfway across the room. He went to a window and stood before it, breathing deeply. Sons of bitches, Brinato thought, pissing their pants over nickles and dimes and a few dead punks, and conniving over what slice of Naples they might or might not get. While we got a *war* on our hands!

Brinato lit a cigar. Well, he thought, they could forget Naples, all of them. Naples is mine. I got my own *boia,* my personal executioner in old Napoli, sorting things out, so Naples don't matter. What matters is that goddam Bolan!

Brinato stared off into the night through the window, eyes going out of focus, trying to envision where Bolan was at that moment, and doing what. . . .

Brinato turned back to the table, picked up his chair, but he did not sit down. He leaned forward on his hands, and once more glared at each of the other men, one by one. "Now! Listen to me. Clear all the cheap penny-ante thoughts out of your minds. All the crap about a slice of Naples, your deads, stolen trucks, *all* that!"

Brinato flicked ashes from his cigar. "First, we *know* why Bolan came over here. We *know* his target." He paused, then growled a grainy coarse laugh. "Does anybody doubt now we *are* dealing with Bolan? Anybody got more smart ideas about taking down one of our *own?* It's Bolan and he raped us blind, so now let's get the son of a bitch."

Then with a deceptive mildness that held a sneer of contempt, Brinato said, "Okay? That okay, boys? Anybody disagree?" He had deliberately taken control of the table because he had been the first to call for a vote at Frode's table. For years Brinato had coveted Naples, especially after his recent probes into the territory verified that Frode's underbosses were stealing him blind and Astio Traditore undercutting him more each day, getting ready to make his move for the takeover. And Brinato had already given his best hardman, his *boia,* the contract on Astio. Bolan, however, had solved that minor problem.

"Okay, who's been in touch with Cafu?" Ricercato asked. "Besides myself, I mean?"

The men from Palermo, Reggio, Messina, Syracuse, and Marsala signified they had been in touch with the boss of Agrigento.

"So what do we know?"

"The truck was found abandoned on the road west of Naro." Ricercato glanced at the truck's owner. "Forget recovering it, unless you're in the junk business."

Paffuto winced, seven thousand U.S. dollars shot to hell.

"What about this crate he was so anxious to move?" Brinato asked.

"His warchest, gotta be."

"Meaning just what?" asked Ruvido. He always was a dumbutt. It took his kind of coarse, heavy-handed, harsh leadership in a sinkhole like Reggio, but that didn't make him any smarter.

"His weapons," Brinato said.

"What the hell," Ruvido said, looking around, "the guy plays cowboy, wears a couple pistols, one with a silencer. What weapons? Was that damned box full of ammo?"

With disgust, Brinato moved away from the table again, puffing furiously at his cigar. "Somebody clue this rural asshole so we can get on with it."

Ricercato began counting off on his fingers. "In the past Bolan has used bazookas, trench mortars, rifle grenades, telescopic rifles, every known kind of demolition explosives, automatic and semi-automatic machine-pistols, rifles, submachineguns. He's an *expert* with them all. You dig, all. THAT's what is in the warchest. Weapons for making war."

"Jesus, then he could stand off, I mean, like way up in the hills somewhere, and rip off Cafu's place."

"What the hell do you think he did in Naples, walk up

to the front door and start lobbing those grenades in? Where the hell you been the past four, five years, while this Bolan bastard's been blowing this thing of ours to smithereens from France to Philly?"

"Well, Jesus, I just never figured, you know—*here!* I mean the guy don't even speak the language, does he?"

"The girl said he speaks some. Enough. Wouldn't you say enough? He went through *your* town, sacked out in a hayloft all day, got himself laid, walked down to the beach in *your* town, and swam out to meet the ferryboat coming in. I think he does okay with the goddamn language!"

"That's right," Brinato said with ice-throated anger. "Bicker, snarl and snap at one another, piss away the whole night."

"Okay, okay. Brinato's right. Now, what's the plan?"

Brinato pointed his cigar at the various dons who had been in contact with Cafu. "What's the man want?"

Each of them shrugged, mouths turning down at the corners, palms up and open. "Nothing?" Brinato said, startled. "Nothing at all? No soldiers, no weapons, ammunition, a goddam helicopter, bloodhounds, *nothing?*"

"That's what the man said," Ricercato said, and looked to the other Sicilian bosses for confirmation.

"That can mean only one thing," Brinato said.

"We think so, too."

"He's got something going over there on his own, something he's not sharing, holding out for himself."

"Well, he's got that soldier thing, training soldiers and sending them over to the other side, for a grand a day per man."

"I know about that, and it was never cleared through the *commissione*. They voted it down cold. Too much chance returning to the old days, Families blowing each other to pieces. We don't never want another bloodthirsty son of a bitch like Anastasia in charge of *anything* again. Murder, Incorporated, *keyrist!*"

"Dope," said the man from Milan. He was nearest France, dealt more than any of the others with the Corsicans. "He's in dope, if he don't want any help, don't want any of us sniffing around. Dope."

Without exception the men around the table agreed, with a nod, a grunt, a word. Brinato laid it out. "Sure. Why not? Some way, Cafu's got a lock on getting his soldiers into the States, right? I mean seventy-five guys he already had in Philly, right? Only makes sense he would send dope with some of them. That's too good a chance to pass up."

Brinato looked around at the faces, saw the grim lines, thin-lipped mouths, stony eyes. "I'm calling a table for Cafu . . . with your agreement, naturally."

Again, without dissent, all the dons agreed.

Brinato went to the door and opened it. He spoke briefly to the man on guard just outside. The soldier nodded and walked away fast. Brinato called out and another man came to the door. A few minutes after Brinato resumed his seat, the door opened and white-jacketed men rolled in tables laden with food and drink.

Even as they dug in, eating and drinking with relish, small-talking and making gross jokes, each man at the table was thinking the same thing. "Officially" their thing had outlawed dealing in dope; dope was too hot now, much, much too heavy. Dope had brought down Don Vito Genovese, for Christ's sake, *the boss* of all bosses. Each man at the table also knew he had at one time or other violated this "ruling" against dope. It was the fastest and easiest way to make a big score if a guy suffered losses and reverses in some other thing he had going. The morality of dealing in dope had nothing whatever to do with laying off dope. Dope was just too goddam heavy if a guy got taken down. And when one guy

134

went down, everyone in the organization suffered, guilt by association, and heat all over the place, cops running out your ears. So, dope was "officially" outlawed in the Mafia, but it was okay so long as you did not get caught.

And the men at the table were also thinking one other thing, everyone of them: how to get the big slice, maybe all, of Agrigento when they called the table on Cafu and took him down.

Brinato's soldier came fast into the room without knocking, leaned over and whispered in his boss' ear. Brinato spluttered a mouthful of food down his chest, slapped at it angrily with his napkin, swallowed heavily, and shoved back from the table. "What did you say? I mean repeat it for all of us."

"Now, boss, don't get sore at me, okay?"

Brinato shook his head violently.

The soldier stared around the faces, shrugged, then blurted, "Don Cafu said . . . 'Tell those guys to go get fucked. And tell them if they come after me I got better'n a hundred soldiers waiting for them.'" The soldier grabbed an empty glass and poured himself a drink of champagne. "He said, 'Tell those greaseballs to go piss up a rope, and if they think they're calling a table on me they're full of shit. I ain't coming, now or ever, and I'll burn down every son of a bitch comes after me.'"

The soldier did not bother with the glass this time. He up-ended the bottle and swigged. Then: "I'm sorry, boss; but that's what he said, just how he said, and I thought you want to know. I mean, did I do right?"

"Sure, sure," Brinato said absently, nodding his head. He patted the soldier on the arm. "You did just fine, son. Go on now, we got to talk. Tell the waiters to come in and clear away all this crap. I ain't hungry no more."

After the waiters had taken away the remains of the feast, which now tasted like sawdust to the dons, Ruvido snarled viciously. "Okay, so the don don't come to the table, we take the table to the don, huh?" He looked around the table for confirmation.

Brinato looked at the man from Reggio, wondering. How the hell did we ever let him get so high up in this thing of ours? A goddam Calabrian was no different than a garlicky greaseball Sicilian, hot-tempered, fast-draw, shoot from the hip, examine the deads afterwards, and hold a beautiful wake upon learning he'd killed his brother-in-law. Christ. Maybe it was the sun, the harsh, unrelenting heat on the jagged desertlike, worthless land made them that way. All the same, kill, kill, kill, and they'd screw anything from a crocodile to a warm exhaust pipe. Sure, Cafu had to go, no question; but Brinato decided Ruvido also had to go. And then he caught himself. God-DAMN! Here he was doing just exactly what that Bolan bastard wanted. Thinking of killing Family. Brinato took a deep breath and calmly peeled the outer brown wrapper from a Cuban cigar and lit it. After a moment, he leaned forward, cleared his throat loudly to quiet the mutterings around the table. When he had the attention of all the dons, Brinato spoke:

"All right, gentlemen, what do you think of this? Our brother Don Cafu does not want our help. He has, indeed, re*fused* our offers of aid. He has likewise refused to come and reason with us. And our only purpose was to offer aid and assistance, correct, gentlemen?"

They nodded, grunted, and most of them began slowly smiling.

"Then I suggest we let the don have his way. Obviously, he considers himself in no danger. A hundred trained and well-armed soldiers, correct? So what can one man hope to do, even this Bolan?"

Brinato puffed his cigar in the silence, while the others watched him, grinning like sharks. "Of course, there are always the pieces to pick up afterwards." Bri-

136

nato smiled, a brief lifting of the left corner of his thick lips. "I suggest we adjourn and see what the morrow brings."

Still grinning, the others got to their feet as Brinato rose from his chair. "Now, let's see if we can't find a way to divert ourselves, eh?"

As they filed out of the table room, Brinato signaled to his houseman. The hardguy grinned and nodded and went away. As the dons went into the lavishly furnished private parlor, soft music began issuing from hidden speakers, the lights softened, and the girls came in.

15: SCOUT

Mack Bolan, The Executioner, was not only a highly efficient practitioner but also a student of military tactics and strategy.

The oldest rule in the book had never changed:

"You must take the high ground,
or you will die in the valleys."

And wars had been lost because of laziness.

Occupying the high ground took men of stamina, will-power, and commitment. Bolan had discovered in his first day's recon that Cafu's trainees had little else on their minds but $1000 a day and easy living Stateside. They did not like to climb mountains, so they faked it. They did not like roughing it, so they lugged along ten pounds of crap in their rucksacks—liquor, canned foods, reading material, and a few even managed to inveigle some of the local girls to come along and spend the watch with them.

In that first day, Bolan could have killed nineteen of Cafu's soldier trainees.

But that would only have set the hounds upon him. When the relief men came up to take their positions on the outer rim of the defense perimeter, and found deads, Cafu would have been alerted and doubly defensive.

Bolan kept scouting, and just before noon he located at last what he sought: a soldier trainee who looked like Mack Bolan. Not really, but perhaps enough. Enough so Mack could take the guy down, replace him, hopefully pass himself off as the soldier long enough to get inside.

If his estimate of the reliefs was correct, he would arrive at the base camp near dusk, and in the gloom possibly pass himself off as the trainee.

First, the trainee.

Mack simply circled down through a deadspace where the soldier could not see him, hit the too-well-worn path leading to the observation post, and walked right up to the soldier. The soldier was asleep, a skin-magazine lying across his chest. Bolan kneeled beside the man, chopped him across the throat, drove the larnyx into the man's throat, then held the man down while he suffocated.

Bolan lifted the man up and threw him over his shoulder, carried him a mile farther back up into the mountains, stripped off the "uniform" Don Cafu's trainees wore, then dropped the body down the shaft of an abandoned sulphur mine. Hundreds of such shafts were in view all through the terrain. At one time, sulphur export had made Agrigento one of the most important cities on the island, with a population of half a million people in over forty villages and the capital city bearing the same name as the province, Agrigento.

The uniform did not fit, but it would do; it had not fit the other guy either, being to large for him, and too small for Bolan. But their coloring, general build, enough the same in general so Bolan believed he could pull it off.

Mentally, he shrugged. If he failed, he would have to shoot his way clear, then outrun them. He went back to the OP and waited, lunching sumptuously on chow the now-dead man had carried on his back up the mountain-side. A hunk of fresh bread, even fresher cheese, a big cut of roast highly seasoned, a water bottle full of excellent white wine. The guy even had American cigarettes, two packs of Camels. Mack lit up and settled back to watch the trail after he'd eaten.

He wondered what the man's name was. There had been no papers on him. Probably Cafu and his organization were taking care of manufacturing/counterfeiting a new identity.

Meantime, though, the dead man had answered to some name, had some identity to his fellow trainees. Then Bolan remembered the sign on a wall in Philadelphia:

SPEAK AMERICAN
THINK AMERICAN
BE AMERICAN

That could be his passport into the alien land.

His relief came an hour before dusk. Bolan heard the man thirty minutes before he saw the *malacarni* come into view down the trail. If they were all as clumsy and club-footed as this dude, then *malacarni* was a misnomer—a real badass does not fall and flounder and puff'n huff so a potential enemy can hear him coming a half-hour before he arrives.

Yet Bolan did not lower his guard.

Overconfidence had killed more men than caution ever would.

Standing fifty yards down the trail, the soldier paused. Bolan saw the sweat-soaked uniform, the heaving chest, the sagging shoulders, and Bolan shook his head. Cafu

141

was selling shit for steel if this dude represented what he hired out for a grand a day.

The man down the trail, standing in plain view, called out hoarsely. Bolan did not understand the word. He had anticipated this. In thickly accented English, Bolan replied, shouting, "We have orders! Spik Eenglish! Training!"

Bolan got to his feet, but remained crouched, waved his left arm, "Come on up!"

Without a pause, the man resumed his climb. Bolan had long been ready to move, and once the man began climbing, Bolan went down the trail fast, and passed his relief before the man knew what had happened, calling out, "Hey, Gino—"

Bolan kept moving until he rounded the first bend in the trail, then he ducked for cover and stripped off his gear, wormed back around to a place of observation and looked up at the OP through his powerful Navy binoculars.

The exhausted *malacarni* lay on his back, shirt unbuttoned, belts and packstraps unfastened, heaving. Bolan got back into his gear and went on down the trail.

Dusk settled quickly in these mountains.

As in every battlefield Mack Bolan had ever seen, known or read of, there was a central dispersal point between homeplate and outposts. In the dusk, with his phenomenal night vision, Bolan spotted the bare spot on a knoll about 700 yards down his trail before he got there. He faded off into brush and knelt behind a huge boulder, pulled out the night binoculars and glassed the meeting spot.

He felt all his combat senses warn him when he saw the big man with a clipboard awaiting the incoming watches from the outposts. The man had too many familiar moves, too self-assured, too much command presence. At one time or another, somewhere, the man with the clipboard

142

had fought with United States military forces. Bolan knew he had as much chance getting past that dude while impersonating the *malacarni* he'd killed as he had shoveling snow in hell.

All right, Bolan thought, it did not work.

So what next?

Let's wait and see.

One by one, the big stud down there checked the men off as they came in, spoke briefly to each one, then sent them on down the mountain.

From his scout, Bolan knew there were eleven high outposts. Six men had been checking in when Bolan came down and began watching. Seven and eight came in almost simultaneously. Nine right behind them. Ten was very late, and it was so dark by then Bolan had to use the Navy glasses' maximum power to watch. Ten was drunk, and the big man awaiting him simply drew a trenchknife also equipped with studded brass knucks and broke the drunken *malacarni's* face to pieces, fast, rapid-fire, professional punches, six of them before the soldier could fall.

Part of being a superior combat tactician meant Bolan was an opportunist. He drew the Beretta, screwed the silencer down tightly, left his hiding post and walked down the trail. He ambled along humming aloud, and as he neared the big man with the clipboard, Bolan heard him say, "Oh, for Christ's sake! Another lousy drunk."

Bolan watched the man draw the knucks-equipped trenchknife. Then Bolan stopped and gestured out side-ways with his left hand. The man automatically turned his head to look and Bolan shot him, sending a 9mm Parabellum slug straight into Eddie The Champ's heart.

Bolan collected the brass hull from his shot and ran to the body of the beaten soldier, jerked the man's Beretta from its holster, removed the clip, thumbed out the top round, checked to see if the chamber was empty, replaced the clip and jacked a round into the chamber. Then he put the gleaming empty brass in the center of the path so it would show and be found easily.

Fast, Bolan went past the dispersal point and down the main trail toward the training camp. He went less than a mile and found the whole setup inside a grove of trees, well camouflaged, even from the air with netting. They had the whole works: firing ranges, obstacle course, barracks, a chow hall, even a small outdoor PX where the soldiers could buy beer, sit at picnic tables, and drink.

Bolan went back up the trail, removed the silencer from the Beretta, fired a single shot into the air, stomped his brass out of sight under a bush, then pulled off to wait. In a few minutes a "patrol" came up the hill. He supposed that was what they would call it, pretend it was, a patrol. It was really five guys crowded together, half-jogging, talking, making noise enough for a full company of raw recruits.

He stayed out to the side, slipping through the bush while the patrol went up the trail. Then they found the two bodies, and the chattering became a loud shouting match. From what Bolan understood, there was no one man clearly in command and the "soldiers" were arguing about what should be done. Mack could not help but think of them in quotes, with contempt, as "soldiers." And had he been careless enough to leave any sign, any evidence of his own presence there, the dumb bastards wiped it out by walking all over it. One of them only found the empty shell casing after he stepped on it, then bent down and picked it up, destroying any fingerprints that might have been on it.

Bolan circled higher, up around to the trail he should come down from the outpost where he left the dead man, and in the almost full darkness he eased in among the men unnoticed. No one seemed to know for sure what to do, so Bolan took command, growling with heavy accent, "How many times you gotta be told, hah? Speak English, speak *American!*"

"Hah, Gino, thatsa you, eh?"

"What's going on here?"

"We trying to figure."

"Who got'm a light?"

"You know the rules," Bolan growled.

He knelt, and then said, "Hell, they fight, look. Smell."

Two of the men dropped to their knees beside Bolan. "Shhh. Get that! Drunk again," said one man. The other said, "Eddie beat him up bad, looka his face, Francesco got no face left."

"But he hadda gun. No more Eddie The Champ. Phutt!"

"Okay," Bolan said with authority, getting to his feet, "we better take'm in."

Without comment, two men got hold of Francesco's feet and started dragging him on his back down the trail. Two others following, dragging Eddie The Champ. Bolan fell in behind them.

Once back to the training compound, Bolan peeled off and while the barracks emptied and lights came on and men with lanterns and flashlights came running to see the sights, Bolan completed his recon of the site.

He located the armory, the food staples storehouse, the supply house with clothing, socks, shoes, other personal gear; then he found one of the two main objectives, the identity manufacturing shop.

There was no guard at the door. Bolan slipped silently inside. An old man wearing thick glasses sat humped over a drawing board, a dazzling light shining on the work in his hands. Bolan watched him for a moment; the man was an artist. Bolan slipped back out, resumed his search, and at last found the ammo dump, his other main objective.

All during his recon, Bolan had kept mental notes, drawing a mental map, counting his steps between each building and establishment. Once he had it down, he widened his search, looking for Don Cafu's headquarters.

He found another trail leading on down toward Agrigento. An on-shore breeze occasionaly carried the odor of the sea to Bolan's nostrils. The trail led to a dirt road and Bolan went on. The road made a turn, and ahead, Bolan saw the huge house, well-lighted. He stopped for a check. At least five men roved the grounds, carrying submachineguns.

Now, what the hell! thought Bolan, having no way of knowing Don Cafu had rebelled against his fellow bosses and the hardmen were not prowling to stop Bolan, but possible assassins sent by the other dons.

As he watched, Bolan saw a flaw in the way the guards patrolled the grounds. Bolan stripped off his *gradigghia* uniform, slipped the Beretta rig back on, fitted a full clip into the butt, then moved like a shadow in his black combat garb.

Bolan moved to within a dozen yards of the place he'd chosen to penetrate Don Cafu's home grounds when someone shot him in the back.

16: PREY

At the sound of gunfire just outside his home, Don Cafu felt his heart leap into his throat. He ran toward the door leading down into the fortresslike cellar, yelling at his inside hardmen, "What was it, what was it?"

"I'll check," said Tony Guida, finding himself swallowing heavily.

"Where's Eddie?" Cafu demanded. "I want Eddie!"

"He's up the hill, boss; you know that. With the troops."

"Get him down here. Right away. You call up there and get him down here right away."

"Sure, boss, if you say so," said Tony, not moving toward the intercom box hooked to a battery-powered line connecting the house with the *malacarni* camp. Tony had long since intended himself as Eddie The Champ's replacement. Champ. Of what? The slob worked his ass off with those greaseballs trying to make soldiers of them and

147

he still looked like a blivit, two pounds of shit in a one pound bag.

"It sounds okay out there now, boss," Tony said. "Why don't I have a look-see, huh?"

An idea sprang full-blown into Tony's head. One of the outside men was a hype, a creep Tony called Riarso because the creep was always licking his lips like he was thirsty, dry-mouthed. Riarso would do anything Tony Guida told him; he would squat and crap on his own heels if Tony Guida ordered him, then lick his heels clean; because no one else in the crew besides Tony Guida knew the creep was a hype and Tony his connection. Tony decided that tonight Eddie The Champ was going to get his ass blown off—accidentally. Riarso was going to make a mistake in the dark, and with his chopper cut Eddie The Champ in half. Accidentally.

Tony consoled his boss again. "Easy, boss, huh? Just keep it cool and let me check around." Tony turned toward the front door, taking up his own Walther P38 machine-pistol. At that moment, the intercom speaker squawked to life. "Boss! Hey, boss! Anybody there, hey, you! Tony!"

"Quit yelling, you dumb bastard," Tony said, striding to the intercom and pressing the lever.

"Okay, look, we got trouble up here, bad, Tony. Real bad."

"So what's the trouble."

"Is the don there?"

"Yeah, he's here. Quit farting around," Tony commanded, watching Don Cafu come slowly back into the room.

"Jeez, Tony. Tony, Eddie's dead, he's shot, he's dead as hell, Tony."

"I heard you the first time, dumbutt. Dead how? What the hell happened?"

"Bolan," said the don; it came out as a squeak.

148

"No," said the voice on the intercom. "It was Francesco."

"Francesco!" Tony Guida shouted. "You're outta your friggin skull."

"No, no, listen. Francesco, he's been carrying wine up with him on watch, and today he must've come in drunk. Eddie beat his face off, but Francesco got off a shot. I mean we checked the pistol and everything, Tony."

Jeeez-uss, thought Tony Guida, how much luck could a guy *have?* The bastard I want hit so I can take over gets blown up while I'm sitting here with the boss, and I don't have to trust a lousy goddam junkie on the job.

Eddie pressed the lever. "Okay, cool it, huh? Now, who's in charge up there?"

"Well, no one, I guess. Gino was sort of taking over, I mean, you know he did some army."

"Okay, let me talk to him."

"Well, that's what I mean. He ain't here. I think he was coming down to report in, you know, about Eddie."

A huge sigh of utter relief gushed from the don's lips, and Tony watched the old man slack into a chair, wiping his sweaty gray face.

"Well," Tony said flatly, "you better take charge yourself, because I got a feeling Gino ain't coming back. We just had some gunfire down here, and I think one of our outside men took Gino down."

Tony paused a moment, thinking, totally aware of the don watching him. He had to make a good impression, and he had to do it now, in a crisis, while the don watched. No one ever knew what that blank-faced, conniving, ruthless old bastard was thinking. He may have had someone else already picked out to replace Eddie, if Eddie ever got blown up; so I won't get a better chance to show my stuff than right here, right now.

Tony pressed the lever. "Okay, do this. Tell the troops

I said you're in charge till I get up there. Get the cooks to put out a good meal, I mean *good;* and plenty of wine for everyone. Get something going up there, card games, anything, I'll send for some girls. Just get to work smoothing it all out, settle everything down up there and I'll do the rest."

"Sure, okay, Tony. You, ah, you taking over for Eddie?"

"That's right," Tony Guida said flatly, turning his head and looking at Don Cafu, "I'm taking over for Eddie. I am speaking for the don."

Don Cafu nodded, and he smiled briefly.

Tony felt elation zing through him like a shot of God-power.

"Don Cafu's right here if you want to verify it."

"Hell, no, Tony. You're the man. I'm with you all the way, and don't forget, huh? The name is Giacomo, I mean *Jack* Vincent, huh, Tony. I'm your guy up here."

"Right, Jack, now get your ass in gear and take charge. Anybody gives you any shit, have'm check with me, or the don. But it better be goddam important, like life'r death before they bother the boss."

"No sweat, Tony. Most of the guys are here now, listening."

"Okay, move it!"

"Check, boss!"

Another ambitious son of a bitch, Tony Guida thought, turning from the intercom. But let him work his ass off. Who gets the credit? Me! The don's new right arm. Tony went to Cafu and gently put a hand on the don's shoulder. "Anything I can get you, boss? You okay?"

"You done fine, Tony. You done as good as Eddie."

"Eddie's dead, boss. Dead." Tony spoke flatly, with an edge on the word.

"You're right. Eddie's dead and now I got Tony. I like you Tony, how you handled everything."

"Okay, boss, now I got to check outside, see what to do with that dumbass Gino who got hisself shot, coming down without warning us." Tony picked up his machine-pistol again and went outside, whistling. He had another thing to take care of, too. Anybody who trusts a junkie is crazy; it's crazy even having one around, unless you can use him. With the death of Eddie The Champ, Tony Guida's tame junkie had gone, in a heartbeat, from an asset to a very distinct liability. Tony wouldn't last ten seconds in his new job if the old man, or *anyone*, discovered he'd been supplying Riarso with morphine.

Well, never put off till tomorrow . . . no time like the present . . . and all that old shit. . . .

Only the last slug of the three-shot burst got Bolan, and he went down, partly from the shocking impact of the slug, but mainly because the shots had come from so close. How in *hell* had he let that happen! He cursed himself.

His back felt afire, but he did not feel anything loose or busted apart inside himself, so maybe he'd had more luck than he deserved. Bolan had no way of knowing he'd been shot only because the hardman was off his post, that he belonged where Bolan had seen the gap in the house-patrol, that he was a junkie nicknamed Drymouth, and that Riarso had sneaked away from his post to give himself a jolt of morph and just happened to see Bolan; and with the euphoric high just hitting him solidly, lifting him ten inches off the ground, Drymouth ripped off a burst at the man-sized shadow he saw moving toward the house. Drymouth had to protect the house. Frig that old don. Drymouth had to protect Tony Guida. So he shot whoever he thought he'd seen sneaking up on the house.

Bolan lay on his back and waited, gritting his teeth against the pain. From hunter he had in an instant become prey. He was shot and down, fifty yards from Don Cafu's

151

house. Somewhere in the dark behind him was the man armed with a submachinegun who had shot him. It was miles back to his weapons cache, and the *malacarni* camp lay between him and his heavy weapons. What was it he'd told himself earlier that day? Laziness killed more men than caution ever did. I got lazy. I got overconfident. I walked in like I owned the joint, and got blown up.

Still, Bolan waited, unmoving, breathing shallowly and silently through his wide-open mouth.

Then he heard the shooter coming. Lying on his back, Bolan saw him emerge from the shadows, and Bolan shot Drymouth through the right eye. Riarso took his Last Trip ever. He took an OD of Mack Bolan, The Executioner.

Bolan rolled over on his stomach and shoved up on his knees. The pain in his wound took his breath, and for a moment the pain was so bad Mack Bolan could not believe it. He put the Beretta on the ground, then felt high up under his left arm and around over his back. The slug had gone into the heavy muscle up fairly high, just missing the shoulder blade, then Bolan felt sticky wet on his right wrist, and probed lightly with his fingertips. The bullet must have hit a rib, skittered along it and emerged almost directly under the armpit. There was a small puckered exit hole, slightly shredded at the edges.

Bolan thought, this isn't possible. The brachial artery runs right through there somewhere; it's probably nicked and I'm bleeding to death like a faucet inside my body cavity. Bolan remained there on his knees, waiting for the dizziness, the faintness preceeding death. Nothing happened . . . except the excruciating pain that went on and on and on.

Bolan retrieved the Beretta and knee-walked to the dead.

He searched the man, astonished to find two morphine syrettes wrapped in a handkerchief in one pocket, exactly the same kind of syrettes used by combat medics. Bolan did not hesitate. The pain was too bad. He could not hope to function, keep his senses clear and alert while fighting such intense pain. He peeled back his left sleeve, made a fist, felt with his fingertips and found the vein, slipped the needle in and squeezed the small plastic container, shooting the morphine into his bloodstream.

Within a minute, Bolan felt the pain diminish enough so he could think past it. He also felt drowsy, but knew he could overcome that. He dropped the remaining syrette into one of the leg pockets of his blacksuit in case he absolutely had to use it later on.

Bolan took a compress from his combat med-kit, put it over the bullet-exit hole and clamped his left arm down over it; he put another compress on the hole in his back. With his right hand, Bolan slipped the dead man's belt from the body, then the necktie. Holding his arm clamped to his side, but leaving his left hand free, Bolan tied the belt and tie together, fashioned a loop, slipped it over his head, fitted it across both compresses, then drew it as tight as he could stand, mashing the bandages into place over the wounds. For a moment he rested there on his knees, head hanging, dripping sweat, muzzy and faint. He'd have given almost anything for a cigarette, and the safety in which to enjoy the smoke.

He holstered the Beretta and drew the dead's submachinegun to him, an MP40/1 Erma—9mm Parabellum full automatic, fitted with a folding stock made of two metal rods and a buttplate. When full, the long box magazine held thirty-two rounds, so it should still have twenty-nine loads in it, Bolan thought. Even many would-be experts called this weapon a Schmeisser machine-pistol, but it was an Erma even though some of the million-plus made during World War Two had been turned out by Schmeisser under subcontract. Bolan found two more full magazines and slipped them into his carrying pouches just as the front door of the big house flew open and a man stepped out, shouting, "Who shot? Who fired those rounds?"

No one answered and the man shouted again. "Check in, by the numbers!"

To Bolan's surprised pleasure, the man shouted in English, and the answers came back likewise. At least some of them were studying their English: Post One, okay; Post Two, okay. . . .

At Post Three the answers stopped. Tony Guida cursed, then shouted viciously, "Riarso, you son of a bitch! Answer up!"

Bolan knew then who'd shot him, who'd he'd killed, whose Erma he now held.

Guida called for Four, Five and Six, and the soldiers answered at once. "Okay, scout around. That stupid goddam Riarso shot one of the soldiers coming down from camp, so fan out and find them. The soldier's name is Gino, maybe's he's still alive."

"Hey, Tony," one of the guards called, "you wanna use the jeep?"

"No, you lazy shit, I don't wanna use the jeep. Find that Gino first, dumbhead, scout up the road. I'll *personally* take care of that buttfaced Drymouth."

Mack Bolan could hardly believe his luck, except he'd *made* his luck.

Muttering curses, the hardmen left the house grounds and came out to the road, formed a loose line across it and the drainage ditches, and began moving toward the camp. Bolan watched them go, but he kept track of them by their shouting back and forth even after they vanished in the darkness.

Bolan sprinted across the road and the grounds and came to a halt in the shadows of the house, back pressed against the ancient stone wall a few feet from the front door.

This was not how he'd planned it, but now he had a target of opportunity.

The target of opportunity.

Inside this house, protected by at least one, but probably no more than three hardmen, was the man Bolan had come to Agrigento to kill. The man who'd put a whole new face on "this blessed thing of ours"; training hitmen, assassins, enforcers, ruthless *malacarni* who could turn the streets of any American town into a vicious, deadly jungle. Men who could turn back the clock in the States, so that parks, and front lawns and streets became open fire-fields between warring factions. Some dream Frank, The Kid, Angeletti had for himself, seeing himself as Scarface Al Capone, ruling whole cities by armed force, so powerful even the police became powerless—the corrupt bought off, the straight cops blown up.

Bolan slipped to the corner of the house. In the back yard, beside an old-fashioned barn with stone walls and a tiled steep roof, stood a U.S. military jeep. Bolan grunted with satisfaction. If he took the house down quick, fast, right, it wouldn't be so far back to his heavy weapons cache. Now he had wheels.

Bolan stepped out of the shadows and banged on the front door with the Erma muzzle, shouting, "Hey! Tony! Open up! We got Gino!"

Bolan waited. He heard heels rapping across the tile floor inside. The door snapped open. Tony Guida stood with a scowl on his face, snarling, "You don't have to wake the whole fu—"

Tony's voice trailed off into choked silence, jaw hanging. Then, as though he finally remembered, his right arm jerked, pulling the P38 machine-pistol up.

Bolan shoved the muzzle almost against Tony's head and pressed the trigger. Ten slugs made obscene wallpaper of Tony Guida's brains and skull and scalp.

Bolan stepped over the body, crouched and ran down

the short hallway to an open door on the left. He shoved the submachinegun around the doorframe and ripped off the last nineteen rounds in the clip, dropped the gun and leaped into the room unsheathing both the Automag and Beretta.

Don Cafu looked almost like a withered old woman as he sat frozen with fear in his big chair, staring, unblinking. Without a touch of remorse, Bolan sighted the .44 Automag and blew the don's head off, literally. The cannonlike impact of the big slug took Cafu just under the chin, drilling through the soft skin of his throat, exploding against his neckbone, shredding the muscles and flesh. The head slammed against the high back of the chair, bounced up into the air, came down and landed in Cafu's lap. The pale, thin old hands gripped convulsively, so Cafu held his own head tightly in his own lap, as though demonstrating the most fantastic parlor trick of all time to guests who had failed to show up for the party.

This would show them, the death-grimaced face seemed to say, eyes bulging, lips drawn back, upper denture plate slipped half out, covering the lower lip.

Then Bolan heard the house hardmen returning. One, then another shouted, and one of them fired at a shadow. Bolan ran back to the hallway, then to the front door. He slammed it shut, took a grenade from his belt, pulled the pin, placed the grenade against the door and slid a hatrack over to hold the grenade in place. He rolled Tony's body over, put another grenade under him, pin pulled, then let Tony's weight back down to hold the spoon in place. He scooped up Tony's P38 after holstering the .44 Automag. He sheathed the Beretta and recovered the submachinegun, pushed the release and dumped the empty clip, shoved in a fresh one as he ran down the hallway to the back door. He threw the back door open and shots shattered wood around the frame. Bolan backed up, found

156

a small table, pulled it forward, then lifted and hurled it out the door. He saw the muzzle flash from one hardman's chopper, sighted and ripped off two three-round bursts. The gunman screamed, came staggering out of the shadows gripping his chopper convulsively, spraying bullets in every direction as he spun and finally fell, dead.

Bolan heard others at the front door. He moved behind a wall, heard the crash as the hatrack went flying as the hardmen kicked in the front door, and Bolan counted silently to himself: one thousand and one, one thousand and two, one thousand and the grenade exploded.

Bolan heard the screams. He crouched and looked around the edge of the wall. A bloody arm, sheared off at the elbow, shot past him.

The concussive force of the first grenade had lifted Tony Guida's body enough so the spoon flew and ignited the detonator of the second frag. Two more gunmen, not killed by the first blast, charged into the house and down the hallway. The second grenade went off directly under the first man, shrapnel and concussion literally splitting him in half from the crotch up.

The second man was knocked back and down, but he was as tough as he hired out to be. Shaking his head, wiping blood from his eyes that came from a scalp wound, he lunged to his feet. Bolan snap-drew the Automag and blew a hole through tough-guy's chest.

He had two grenades left. He pulled the pins on both, flung one down the hallway to bounce out the front door and wheeled and underhanded the last through the back door.

The first went and he heard screams. Then the second went and while sizzling hot shrapnel still razzled through the air, Bolan charged out the back door, spraying with the P38 until it emptied and he threw it. Never slowing, Bolan hosed the Erma in sweeping arcs. A huge slug of adrenaline hit him and he ran with his feet hardly touching ground. He leaped over the front end of the jeep, its windshield folded down, and landed in the seat. It needed no key, the military model, probably stolen during that last big war, and he started it.

A huge fire had started in the big house and everything became as light as day, with a yellowish glow. A burst of fire ripped into the rightside seat of the jeep. The hardmen searching for Gino had come running back when Bolan hit the house. Bolan jerked the jeep into low, raced the engine and popped the clutch. He held the Erma by its pistolgrip, extended metal stock's buttplate jammed against his bicep.

A man rose from hiding on the roof, sighted, and Bolan poured a five-round burst of 9mm Parabellum chest dissolvers into the hardman. He reared straight up, and for a moment stood there, then fell forward dead, still clutching his own Erma in his right hand.

Two more armed men ran from the door at the end of the barn as Bolan wheeled around in a circle. Still holding the Erma one-handed, buttplate braced, Bolan drove with his left hand. He emptied the magazine at the two men, saw them staggering and going down as he cleared the yard and drove careening past the fire-roaring big house, dropped the submachinegun in his lap and used both hands to take the corner onto the road leading back toward the soldiers' camp.

He roared into the camp and, for a moment, thought he might pull off a headlong surprise rush and make it through unrecognized, or too fast for any reaction.

He almost made it, but then someone opened up with a long burst. The first rounds went high, *crack!*-ling overhead. Then Bolan felt and heard slugs hit the back of the jeep. The spare tire blew up with a *pow!* that made him jump outside his skin. Then another burst got both back tires and the jeep slewed around, almost overturning.

Bolan dived clear and ran, hearing the voices of the soldiers from camp.

The belt or the necktie had broken, the compresses were gone from his wounds. As he ran, Bolan tasted his own blood spraying into his face. It were as though he drank his own life.

He kept running, once more the prey, not the hunter.

17: STALK

Brinato hung up the radio telephone and closed the door of the safe in which he kept the ultrasecret "hotline" in his Roman villa.

He turned to his *boia,* Razziatore. "Get the helicopter."

The assassin, who looked like a pink-cheeked all-American college lad, nodded without speaking and went to a desk with four telephones. He picked up the green one, after a moment said, "Bring in the ship, full equipment."

That's what Brinato liked most about the lad. No bullshit. No crap about, "What's up, boss?" He told the kid, "Do this, hit that bastard, bring the girl," and Razz nodded, sometimes smiled, especially if it was a hit, and he *did* it. No bullshit. And no bullshit afterwards, either. No preening and strutting around like some peacock with his fan spread. Brinato thought the kid was maybe queer, or asexual so that kind of stuff never entered his mind. Whichever, Brinato knew it never interfered. He'd thought about bringing the kid along, giving him experience in shylocking, numbers, muscle stuff along the docks, bagman for cops on the take, giving him an inside view of everything in this thing of ours, but the kid showed no interest. He was a pure out and out fucking killer and that's all there was to it. He didn't even care about clothes. Brinato wouldn't have been seen *inside* his villa wearing less than half-a-Large worth of raw silk underwear and robe, except when stark naked under the shower; but Razz, Christ, he took any kind of crap off the rack down at the phony high-class clothing shop Brinato had so he could rape the tourists. Trash he wouldn't bury an enemy in, he got two, three hundred bucks (discount for dollars or Deutchmarks) for, because they had counterfeit high-class labels sewed in them. Suckers!

Brinato was dressed in silk almost worth one Large, from the skin out, when he heard the thudding beat of the helicopter blades. He went to the big window and watched the ship settle slowly in atop the reinforced roof of the villa, then said, "Let's go, kid," and they took the elevator up.

According to instructions, standing orders, the pilot had shut down and the blades at rest when the boss and Razziatore came out of the elevator. The boss liked dust blown on him about as well as he liked getting peed on in the face, so the pilot had everything ready—because the boss liked delays even less than he liked dust.

Brinato paused beside the pilot. "You're set, right?"

"Yes, sir!" Donato answered, touching his cap. "The extra fuel tanks topped off, the rockets in place," he touched the seemingly out-sized landing skids which actually served the purpose of being rocket launchers as well as landing gear. "We've got the usual armament aboard. And the other thing, too," the pilot added, swallowing.

"Okay, *that* you get rid of."

The boss had just made the pilot a happy man. Donato drew a fantastic wage, the equivalent of almost three thousand U.S. dollars a week. But there was a catch to it. His work was not only frequently dangerous, often involving the assassin in some way or other; but also in various smuggling operations, sometimes narcotics. Since the helicopter was completely *open*—that is, it was openly registered to Brinato under the name of one of Brinato's many interlocking corporations, the helicopter had a self-contained self-destruct device aboard, just in case it was ever seized by the cops in a smuggling operation, most specifically dope.

The device was absolutely fail-safe, but Brinato still didn't trust it, just as he trusted nothing on earth, not even his wife. That's why he had her run over by a truck four years ago.

It took but a few moments to remove the device, then they were airborne, with the pilot going fullballs on direct course toward Agrigento.

Brinato had neglected to advise his fellow dons of this trip. He would let them in on the action, what was left of it, after he took the lean meat and gravy from the remains of Cafu's operation, said don being now deceased. As he lit a fat Havana, Brinato again congratulated himself for having sent a man over to the island when Cafu failed to show up for Frode's table. The hotline call had given Brinato the Word, and probably a several-hour edge on the other dons. Agrigento was a shambles. Cafu dead, his two main underbosses dead, a bunch of greaseballs running around the hills looking for that Bolan bastard. Meantime, what the hell were the other underbosses doing? The shylockers, bagmen, taxi operators, dock-bosses, whoremasters, olive oil monopoly guys . . . all the real, solid, tried and true and proved moneymakers—

The sons of bitches were stuffing their own pockets, that's what, without a boss of bosses. Piss on that assassin school. What was a grand a day for soldiers? Nothing. Brinato's own numbers syndicate, out of the three poorest most poverty stricken slums in Rome, nickle and dime stuff, made twice that, *net,* on the average. That was *net.* That was *after* paying off a standard ten percent for the runners, *after* fixing the cops, *after* paying off a few winners, unless he'd rigged it so there were no winners. And the goddam payoff wasn't all the way across the goddam Atlantic and Mediterranean, either. On the other side of the world, for Christ's sake! So you looked up some morning with shit on your face because the Angeletti kid didn't pay off and there wasn't a friggin thing you could do about it. It was crazy.

And besides that—

The *commissione* had turned the idea down, absolutely, one hundred percent, unanimously.

All it got Cafu, his big plan, his big moneymaker, was dead. His head in his lap. Brinato shuddered.

You fool, Bolan told himself, you did not come here to die. That's not why you go to war, to die. You go to fight and win, and survive.

He pulled up.

No man on the island was half as physically well conditioned as Bolan. Not even the *malacarni.* They hadn't done their training properly. The outposts he'd scouted out, all of them, had been a mile, sometimes more, farther down the mountain than originally planned and laid out. They had doped off, and now they paid the penalty. They could not overtake Bolan, even when The Executioner was shot to pieces and leaking life from his wounds every step.

He sat down, dragging deep, shuddering painful breaths, getting his wind. He could hear them, far below now, using lanterns and lights, calling back and forth. Once, two groups got into a firefight between themselves. Bolan looked up, got his bearings from the stars, then moved out again, slowly and carefully, conserving himself, and searching.

If the *malacarni* stuck with it, they could still stalk him down, just by following Bolan's spoor—the dripping trail of blood.

Then he found what he sought.

At the base of a bush, he saw a hole, kicked it apart, found the thick spider webs, plastered them over his chest wound. In a few minutes the bleeding stopped. Bolan went on. In an hour he came to the abandoned sulphur mine, his cache. Once inside, he forced open the case of medical supplies and went to work on himself. First a transfusion of albumin to replace lost blood. He bound himself up in tight and proper fashion. He found the bottles and took a handful of vitamin B-12 and almost as many vitamin E pills. He shot a half-million units of penicillin into his butt. He crammed his mouth full of high energy chocolate bar rations, munching as he worked. He went to the mouth of the mine shaft and looked at the sky. He had another four hours till first light. It might be just enough, if he didn't cave in.

Because what he had been through was nothing to what now faced him, Bolan set to it with the professional soldier's understanding and frame of mind.

In combat, more than in garrison, an infantryman is more packmule than fighting man, until the fighting starts. An infantryman carries all he owns, all he needs, on his own back—his chow, his water, his ammo, his weapon, his dry socks and sleeping bag; he is, and he is supposed to be, a self-contained unit with his own life-support system. If he happens also to be a gun crewman, he has the additional load of mortar or bazooka or machinegun ammunition added to his personal load.

Bolan was all of these and more.

With the albumin blood replacement, the antibiotics, the high-energy vitamins and concentrated chocolate steadily revitalizing him, Bolan set to work.

He took the mortars out of the mine shaft first, set the baseplates, sunk the spike-ended bipods in place, laid the tubes. He made another round trip and came back with the ammo and aiming stakes. He unpacked the ammo, laid out all the bomb-shaped, finned shells, and put maximum propellant charges on each shell. These were small bags of gunpowder that fit at the base of the fins and were ignited by the primer, the primer fired by the weight of the shell when dropped down the mortar tube, striking the fixed firing pin. Besides the flesh-shredding HE—high explosive—shells, Bolan had flare shells and one William Peter, a WP, white phosphorous, for marking. The William Peter not only caused casualties, burning fiercely, but it marked targets with a dense white cloud of smoke.

Bolan went back to his cache and brought the M79 grenade launcher up with a case of grenades. He rested then, and listened.

Some of the soldiers had not yet given up; they still stalked him in the night. But their training had been either inadequate or their discipline lousy. They sounded like cattle moving around, and what they thought were low-voiced commands or questions came to Bolan atop the hill as shouts. Had he been capable, Bolan might have felt some pity for them.

He went down and got the Browning, and the ammo.

During his years as a professional soldier, more than ten years including two extended tours in Vietnam where he first became known as The Executioner, Mack Bolan had seen, fired, experimented with, learned to field strip and reassemble, virtually every type of small-arm known to man. As a pro, it was his business to know weapons.

166

He had seen them all, from the most primitive copies made in China and North Vietnam, which were as likely to explode in the gunner's face as kill an enemy, to the most highly sophisticated, particularly including the vastly overrated Swedish weapons. After years of experimentation, and thousands of rounds of ammo fired in practice and combat, Sergeant Mack Bolan arrived at the same conclusion that most combat men eventually did. . . .

Nothing, *nothing,* could beat the BAR.

Range, accuracy, dependability, mobility, every way from dawn till dark and all night long.

Yeah, the BAR had its limitations.

Call them faults, if you're of a mind. So?

The son of a bitch is heavy, sixteen pounds, empty.

Put in a twenty-round magazine and you've got close to twenty pounds, including a stout leather sling. It's long, just an inch short of four feet—forty-seven-inches!

And it shoots .30 caliber ammo, the damned brass big around as your ring finger, and the steel, springload magazines aren't exactly weightless.

But the only thing about it is, Jack, when your ass is in a jam, whether in desert grit and grime, or jungle mud and slime, all you have to do is pull the trigger on a BAR and it will shoot exactly where it's aimed. On full-auto, high-cyclic rate of fire it cranks off 550 rounds per minute. On slow rate, 350 rpm. A man with the touch can shoot it one, two, three, rounds at a time.

The goddam weapon was invented in 1917 and used in World War One!

But nothing yet had ever beat it. Any dogass soldier could pick up a BAR and knock down men at 500 yards. Mack Bolan could bullseye men through the torso at 1500 yards. The BAR's maximum range was 3500 yards, roughly *two miles*.

Long ago, when Mack Bolan set out on his war against the Mafia and "burglarized" a weapons dealer's warehouse (leaving money to pay for his "purchases") it had not been by accident, but by deliberate design that Sergeant Mac Bolan, late of the U.S. Army, chose Browning Automatic Rifles and several thousand rounds of .30 caliber ball and tracer ammo, and a whole sack full of extra magazines, among his primary arsenal.

Bolan could hear the more persistent stalkers now, clearly in the vast, quiet stillness of night atop the Sicilian mountaintop.

It was time to give them something new to think about.

He picked up a heavy HE mortar shell, pulled the arming pin, placed the fins down inside the tube, then let it drop, covering his ears tightly so the firing would not deafen him.

When it hit bottom, the shell primer fired, ignited the increment charges, and with a solid *chuonk!* the round went.

A voice called out. "Hey! Franco, what the hell wasa *that!*"

"I don't know. I think I saw a flash, up above a little."

Bolan squatted on his heels and waited, counting.

He didn't care where the first round hit, all he wanted was the effect, the mental, emotional, *personal* effect.

He counted down, and when his lips silently mouthed *zero,* he saw far below him the bright orange blossom, a gush of smoke, but no sound. He dropped in another round just as the noise of the first explosion washed up the mountainside.

"What the hell was that," the same voice shouted again.

"Some kinda explosion. Christ in all His mercy! *Look!*"

The second round hit and blossomed, like hell rupturing through a fissure in the earth.

"Son of a bitch, he slipped past us and got back inside!"

"No, no, wait. I know that sound. It's a mortar. He's up here, firing a mortar."

"You know *shit!*" Franco answered. "He's back down there. Come on!"

"I know what I'm saying, goddammit. Go if you want but I'm staying. I know."

Bolan thought, you know too much, asshole; so lie down and stop breathing, you're already dead."

He could hear the one man going downhill, fast, crashing through the brush, tumbling stones, calling out, "Come on, come on."

Bolan dropped another round down the tube.

Each time he fired, Bolan not only clamped his hands over his ears, but ducked away and clamped his eyes tightly closed. That a mortar threw no muzzle flash at all was fiction. It blazed enough to blind a careless gunner, and enough to be spotted by a careful observer who knew where to look.

Night vision unimpaired, Bolan drew the silenced Beretta, sat with his elbows locked on his knees and waited for smartguy Franco. He saw the bulky shape appear, and heard the man panting like a hospital case dying of asthma. Bolan let Franco have his small victory. Let him see the firebase Bolan had established. Let him turn, even let him shout, a shout unheard as the third round's explosive noise came rebounding up the mountainside.

Then Bolan shot him three times through the chest, for insurance, not completely certain he'd adequately protected his night vision.

Bolan got up and walked over to Franco and rolled him over and saw he'd wasted two bullets. He dragged the body back to his firebase, laid him down carefully, then unwrapped another chocolate bar and ate it.

18: REVERSAL

From *Journals,* Mack Bolan, The Executioner

*Many times when I go in, I never know how
I will get out, or if I will. More than once in these
pages I've declared myself already dead. All I
care about is accomplishing the mission. Beyond
that nothing matters.*

The central *piazza* of Agrigento was but three miles inland from the seaport of the same name. Around the
town square, as in most cities throughout the world, stood
offices of the local, provincial, and federal governments.
In the office of the Night Chief of Police, sat a man of
great bulk and substance. He wore a uniform, and polished cavalry style boots actually equipped with small
spurs. He wore a Sam Browne style waistbelt and shoulder strap, and a tiny automatic pistol. Above the left
breast pocket of his nicely tailored uniform the man wore

an ornate solid gold, silver inlay, blue and green enameled badge.

The door to the man's office was locked and his telephone off the hook.

It required considerable concentration, but the Night Chief did not heed the pounding on his door, the shouts of the door pounders, or the thin high-pitched squawk issuing from the earpiece of the telephone. Instead, the man read with some relish the latest scandal among the cinema actresses, and licked his lips lasciviously when he looked at highly revealing photos of Sophia Loren.

The Night Chief of Provincial Police was not only aware of what seemed to be happening a few miles outside his city, but had been aware of it for at least thirty minutes before the townspeople. A policeman relied heavily upon informers. Policemen who wished to live good and satisfying lives, grow old, retire gracefully, die in bed of such reasonable ailments as heart disease or other disorders brought on by a lifetime of dissipation did not foolishly rush off into the night when any damned fool with ears knew there was a war in progress at Don Cafu's.

The Chief was fully aware of who and what Don Cafu was and represented. It was, in fact, with the don's blessing, combined with certain arrangements, that the Night Chief got his job, which did not include interfering with happenings of any kind whatever upon Don Cafu's estate. If, upon the morrow, Don Cafu emerged victorious, the Chief had less than nothing to worry about. He would, in fact, be rewarded for not intruding himself into Family matters.

On the other hand, if he learned that Don Cafu had gone down in defeat, the Chief still had nothing to lose. Certainly, the new don would see how wise and provident the current Night Chief of Police was, and would therefore have no reason to wish for a replacement. Certain understandings and arrangements would be made, and things would go on as they had always gone on in Agrigento, Mafialand.

Of course, certain base and faithless persons might jeer at the Chief behind his back, and others possibly find a printing press to run off cowardly caricatures; and without doubt some vile creature would shit on his doorstep or call his wife to accuse him of being a secretive homosexual, but a policeman's lot, as the saying goes. . . .

The one thing the Night Chief was totally unprepared for was the arrival of a sleek turbojet helicopter, letting down directly in front of the police station. At the authoritarian command that he unlock the door, the Chief did so at once. Of course he recognized Signor Brinato at once, but not the smiling youngster who followed the most esteemed Signor Brinato into the office, like a shadow.

Brinato spoke with a voice that sounded like his throat was filled with crushed ice. He complimented the Chief on his behavior. He complimented the Chief upon his willingness to let Family matters sort themselves out. He introduced himself as the new, ah, resident—possibly *in absentia*—of what was formerly known as the Cafu estate. And, of course, all previous, ah, arrangements would continue in effect, until some more convenient time for renegotiation. Did the Chief have any objections?

"Absolutely none and let me be the first to welcome you."

"I thank you. Now, perhaps you could clear this rabble from the streets. The helicopter is extremely expensive, extremely so, and easily damaged."

It was done in minutes, and so was the Chief's personal Rolls Royce Silver Cloud brought around so Signor Brinato might ride to the Cafu—the new Brinato, formerly Cafu, estate.

Bolan heard the chopper pass overhead, and was plain-

173

ly startled to see it circle, then hover, and slowly begin descending over the city.

His first thought was: "Cops!"

His second thought came a fraction of an instant later. It's time to strike. I'm not killing any cops.

He checked the positions of the mortar baseplates, adjusted the sights, dropped the parachute flare round down one tube, and the William Peter down the other.

The flare lighted the whole island, it seemed. The stark bare hills lay naked, the outposts' foxholes, the trails, the old mineshafts. Farther down, he saw the buildings of the *malacarni* camp, and beyond it the big stone house. The WP smoke shell landed sixty yards long. Bolan adjusted the tube, then ignoring his ears, he pulled the safety pins and dropped shells down both mortar tubes one after another as fast as he could. He had twenty rounds in the air before the first hit, landing beside the cookshack door. The explosion tore the whole end off the building. The remainder of the flimsy structure swayed and buckled, swayed, then caved in. Other rounds fell in, *crunch! crunch! crunch!* and an air-whapping wave of sound came up the mountainside, whipping dust into Bolan's eyes.

Small, antlike men ran in all directions. Bolan saw one mortar shell hit a running man in drawers square in the top of the head, and the man vanished.

19: TAKE-DOWN

Bolan worked the sighting screws on both mortars, then again pulled pins and fired as fast as he could, once more putting twenty rounds into the air before the first hit. For a moment he thought the big house was beyond maximum range, or maybe the powder in all the increments was old and he was getting short rounds, because the first three hit along the road between the camp and the house.

Then the others rained down like shooting fish in a rain pond, all seven direct hits or such close misses they whapped the stone walls. But the goddam house refused to fall.

The flare died out and Bolan sat back resting. He lit a cigarette and puffed. He wanted them to think that was it. That it was over, all clear, okay to come out of your holes now, boys.

He rolled over and pulled the BAR to his shoulder, slapped the bottom of the magazine to see it seated firmly, cocked the automatic rifle, and ran off the first magazine, five bursts of three rounds each and a final burst of four, all tracers. He adjusted for a slightly higher angle, changed magazines, then poured it on three, three, three, three, three, four. Changed magazines and repeated it again, and again.

In military terminology it was plunging fire. To the men down there, the bullets seemed to be coming from the sky, coming straight down on them.

Bolan fired his last flare shell from the mortar.

Even as it left the muzzle, he began firing the BAR once more, professionally, methodically. The flare burst open in a hellish green light, and he saw men reeling, frantically rushing in every direction, knocking each other down. A few were shooting, in every direction. Two men seemed to hear gunfire at the same time, wheeled around, and shot each other.

Hellground.

Slaughter in Sicily, right in the Mafia's womb. Where the bastard fathered by terror and birthed by a bitch named expediency had grown to monstrous size and strength, so it could wipe out the family of a professional soldier fighting in Vietnam.

Bolan pulled the bagful of remaining BAR magazines to him and looped the strap around his neck. He slung the M79 grenade launcher across his back. He got the bagful of frags and hefted them on his other shoulder. He pulled the pins on two frags but held the spoons tightly, then dropped them down the mortar tubes. When the surviving *malacarni* came up the mountain and found the mortars, unless they knew their business, there would be more deads. When they tipped the tubes up from the baseplates the grenades would fall free, flip their spoons, and detonate.

But as he dropped the frags down the tubes. Bolan went fast and low down the steepest part of the hill from

176

his fire-base. Those tubes could be hot enough to cook-off the frags and Bolan didn't want his ass full of hot steel.

Bolan skirted the *malacarni* camp, hardly bothering to conceal himself except to stay in the shadows. The camp lay in ruins. The stunned survivors staggered about in a state of shock. No one had made any effort to mount a counterattack.

Bolan still had three objectives before calling the mission accomplished.

Well, perhaps four . . . if he counted on getting away.

But three for sure, first. Then see about getting out.

He found a place offering concealment and good cover behind large boulders, stopped and dropped his heavy load. He unbagged the shotgun-shell propellant charges for the M79 and laid them out in a row on the ground in front of his knees. He loaded the grenade launcher, sighted, and put one into the counterfeit documents shop, then another. The frame building went up in a sheet of flaming kindling.

Calmly, Bolan reloaded, shot down the door of the ammo dump with the first round, laid the second inside, and then he crouched behind the boulders and waited for the secondary.

The ammo dump went like the start of World War Three. When earth, wood, metal, and parts of bodies stopped raining down, Bolan looked over the boulders and saw the armory also flattened and afire. Only a large smoking hole where the ammo had been.

He gathered the remaining gear and slipped on through the shadows. It was beginning to get light. He realized he could see farther, make out distinct shapes rather than darker masses in the dark.

If he wanted to get out, he should go. But he could not stand the thought of leaving without a complete take-down. He wanted to see that goddam house—that . . . that *castle,* yeah, ruler of Agrigento, the late Don Cafu. Bolan wanted nothing left for the sons of bitches to look at but rubble, junk. It's hard to build a legend on trash, difficult to worship the residue of destruction.

He stopped again near the place he had first approached the house. He could see the white shape of Riarso's naked body.

The house was a gutted, still flaming ruin; but it also still stood, big, blocky, stone and mortar, and looking too goddam much like a monument.

Standing in the open, methodically firing one grenade after another with the M79, Bolan sent the stone-crunchers into the foundation, blowing out one corner after four shots, the other after five. He moved farther along so he could see the side of the building. He refused in his mind to call it a home, or even a house, and shot again and again, until his grenades were gone, and the house still stood.

He felt like crying.

He turned to go back to the BAR when a sound slapped past his ear and he whirled around. An ivory white Rolls Silver Cloud came up the paved drive toward the house, and from the back window behind the driver a man was shooting at Bolan.

Bolan dropped, drawing the Automag. He sighted on the driver and squeezed, then threw the shot wide in the last possible instant when a first ray of sun glinted on the badge above the driver's heart. The shot took out the front windscreen of the car and the driver lost control. Bolan fired again and again, punching .44 Magnum holes through every glass of the Rolls.

The door on the far side suddenly flew open and a man leaped out, shouting, *"Bolan! Bolan!* Wait. I want to talk."

"Okay, stand up and talk." Bolan watched from cover.

The big man rose to his feet in his silk suit, brushing at his sleeves.

"Come out and talk." The man gestured. "We can deal, Bolan."

"Who am I dealing with?"

"Police. Get out Chief. Look, Bolan, we can fix this. Goddam you, Chief, get OUT!"

The front door opened and the fat policeman struggled from behind the wheel, gasping so loudly, Bolan may not have heard the command if he had not seen the man in silk also move his lips. *"Now!"*

The back door flew open and a man armed with a shotgun, lying on the floor of the car, let off both barrels at Bolan. One of the slugs caught Bolan below the right knee and knocked him down as he rose. The rest of the deadly double-aught buckshot went wide and low, ripping a long wide hole across the ground.

Bolan discounted the shotgunner. He was an empty gun for the moment. Instead, he shot the burly dude in fancy clothes, through the guts. The .44 Mag folded Brinato in the middle like a wet taco and drove him ten feet backwards until he tripped and fell rolling. He screamed, holding his middle.

"Live with it a while, you mother," Bolan said, "yeah, let's talk." He shot the other man lying on the back floorboard just as the cool bastard shoved in another pair of double-aught loads and snapped the shotgun into battery.

The policeman lay on his side in the dust and Bolan knew he'd finally done it.

Killed a cop.

Stray round, ricochet, whatever. The Executioner would get blamed for it. He dragged the man out of the back and dumped him, dropped a marksman medal on his chest.

"Pleese-a, don't-a keel me, *signor*."

179

Bolan whirled to find the cop on his knees.

"I ain't going to kill you, man . . ." Bolan breathed deeply again. "Unless by accident, when you scare the living crap out of me!"

"Pleese–a–no, I got–a wife three bambin."

"Forget it, man. This your car?"

"Is *your* car, you want. Take, take all. Here, you wanna some mon." The cop dropped his fat moneyclip on the road and pushed it toward Bolan.

"Where's the helicopter?"

"In–a see–tee. You wan?"

Bolan could hardly hear the cop. That Brinato certainly could scream, gutshot as he was.

"Put it away, copper. I don't want your bread." Bolan went to him. "Come on, get up, get–UP!" He jerked and the cop leaped at the same time and Bolan shoved him under the wheel. As they turned and drove down the road toward town, Bolan could still hear Brinato. He certainly could scream. Just went on and on and on, and loud, too. Best screamer I ever heard, Bolan decided.

EPILOGUE

Handling the pilot had been no problem at all. Once airborne, Donato freely admitted that if he'd known Brinato was lying gutshot and dying up at the big house, he'd have taken off on his own. He wanted no friggin' part of that war he could hear going on up there.

"You're Bolan, aren't you?" Donato asked, shooting a look at the blacksuited Executioner while the man strapped a bandage on a flesh wound below his right knee.

Bolan didn't answer.

"You did a hell of a job, guy, I'll say that. For one man, key-rist, you brought it down."

"Not quite." Bolan jerked his chin.

Donato looked past Bolan, and all he saw was devastation. "I don't get you."

"That goddam house is still standing. I shot the damned foundation from under it, but it's still there."

"And it bugs you, huh, bad."

"Real bad . . . but I'll get over it."

Donato tapped Bolan's arm. "Look, what are your plans? I mean, what do I have to look forward to? A hole in *my* guts, too?"

Bolan shook his head: no.

"Okay, then what are your plans. I mean, like, you know, where we going, man?"

"How much fuel do we have?"

Donato didn't answer. He looked at Bolan. After a long moment, Donato said, "You want to deal? I got something you just might go for."

"If it's a trick, let me tell you, the last guy used those words to me was Brinato."

"No way, man." Donato grinned widely. "You want that house down. Okay, dig this, Mack Bolan."

Donato banked the chopper around sharply. He reached up to an overhead panel with a key, unlocked a small door that revealed four switches, the two in the center with red metal safety shields over them. Donato flipped the two unsafetied switches and from the corner of his eye, Bolan saw the front of the landing gear skid peel off and fall away.

When he looked back, Donato had flipped up a plastic plate with gunsight markings on it. He jockeyed the chopper, lowered the nose, increased power, jockeyed again, seemed to settle into a groove, then he said, "Lift the safeties and flip those two switches."

Bolan had caught on by then. He fired the rockets. The house went down like a dynamited smoke stack, flying apart and caving in all at once.

There would be no "monument" to Don Cafu, no Mafia shrine, no basilica for this thing of ours in Agrigento.

"Okay, your deal," Bolan said.

"We've got enough fuel for Algiers." Donato grinned. "They let every other kind of asshole in there, airline hijackers, dope peddlers, Black Panthers, so it's worth a try."

182

"It sure as hell is."

"And I keep the chopper, right?"

"She's all yours, ace. Wake me when we get there, huh?" Bolan crawled into the back seat and stretched out as best he could, bone-ache tired, wounds washing firelike pain across his chest and down his side, along his leg. Yet, Mack Bolan smiled.

God, that was a beautiful sight, watching that house go down. A man didn't get to see one go like that every day.

Beautiful, just beautiful.

Unknown to Bolan, he was spotted in Algiers less than an hour after he arrived. But instead of a battle resulting, the man who spotted him followed new orders, arrived in his office at midday. After locking his office and pulling the shades, he opened his safe. He took out a locked, steel-covered book that was itself a small safe. Laboriously, because he was unaccustomed to such work, the man encoded a message. He locked the book, returned it to his safe and locked the big box, then slipped out the back door of his office and went immediately to the international wireless office. After the message was sent, the man bribed the operator to recover the company copy of the message, then went outside and burned both his handwritten copy and the one he bought.

Less than an hour later a rasping buzzer woke a superbly fit husky man in a lavish home at the foot of the Rocky Mountains outside Denver, Colorado. He came awake fast but unmoving, like a vastly experienced combat infantryman—totally awake, alert, and wary, knowing where his weapons were and which way to go. He reached over and lifted the receiver of the special telephone. "Yes."

"We have an urgent most secret coming in, Mr. Molto."

"Algiers?"

"Yes, Mr. Molto."

"I'll be right down."

Mr. Molto got out of bed. He stood naked in a shaft of moonlight and looked at himself in the full-length mirror on the back of the bedroom door. He stood just over six feet tall and weighed two hundred twelve pounds, every ounce of it bone, gristle, muscle, and jungle instinct. It was the body of a pro football running back in his prime, yet the man's hair was completely gray, close-cropped, and he was past forty years of age. Looking at himself dispassionately, Molto hoped for a moment that he personally had the chance to face Bolan. Man-to-man, he could take Bolan. He could take anyone he'd ever seen. Then Molto dismissed the thought. That wasn't the plan. That was the kind of crap thinking that had allowed Bolan to survive as long as he had.

Molto slipped into socks, loafers, slacks and a golf shirt, brushed his teeth quickly and brushed his hair, then went to the elevator, down, into the new CIC . . . Combat Intelligence Center.

The two men on duty rose to their feet, almost assuming the position of attention. Molto shot a look at them, heads to feet and back again. "You need a haircut, Contabile."

"Yes, sir."

"All in?"

"Yes, sir," the young man needing a haircut said, and he handed a slip of paper to Mr. Molto. Molto nodded and went to a wall safe, shielded the combination lock with his body and when the door clicked open he took out a duplicate of the steel-bound book used by the man in Algiers. Molto also took out a machine that looked somewhat like a combination typewriter-calculator-keypunch machine. He put the machine down on a desk, unlocked the codebook, found the key for the day, jerked his chin, and the young man plugged the machine into an electric outlet.

The message in his hand was in a series of capital letters, all in blocks of four:

ANDE KNBC RORP WMEC USSU AWYC LKER WJSO
GUYM OZWW NMMB DZPB DALW LECM JTDW JOLD
ENDS YMIA

With a dexterous speed that made the two youngsters look at one another and grin sickly, Mr. Molto's fingers flew over the keyboard, feeding input. The machine whirred and clacked, and a few seconds later a strip of paper began emerging from the left bottom side of the decoder. When Mr. Molto finished the serials, he pulled the tape out a few extra inches and tore it off. The young man who needed a haircut unplugged the machine, coiled the cord and put the machine back into the safe, and at a nod he closed the automatically locking codebook and returned it to the safe, then shut the safe and spun the dial.

Molto looked at the message and grunted after reading it through. Without looking up, he said, "Activate the B Team, Red Alert."

"Yes, sir, Mr. Molto," said Contabile.

Mr. Molto, still studying the message, said, "Give me the Hot File."

"Yes, sir, Mr. Molto," the other youngster said and jumped to a filing cabinet, unlocked it, took out a red folder and put it on the desk. Mr. Molto put the tape strip down and let it curl as he picked up the file and opened it. Each page in the file was devoted to a city or an area, and graphically illustrated, daily updated, was a comparison of Family activity in the city/area and the counteractivity of law enforcement agencies. Without looking up, Molto said, "The map."

The far end of the room darkened and then on the wall in full color appeared a map of the United States. Superimposed on the map, at Pittsfield, Boston, New York

City, Washington, D.C., Los Angeles, Chicago, San Francisco, and every other place that bastard Bolan had hit, there was a blood-red B.

"Bastard!" Mr. Molto growled through clenched teeth.

From his console, Contabile said, "Alert acknowledged, Mr. Molto, they want the time."

"Tell them to stand by a few moments," Molto snapped, alternately studying the map and the Hot File. It was an act. He already knew. He just did not want the old men, the nationals to think it too easy. He knew the duty man on the other end of the line with Contabile was already in the act of notifying *La Commissione* that Molto had called a Red Alert and activated the B Team.

Mr. Molto closed the file and said, "Map off." The room brightened again and the picture faded. Molto looked at his wristwatch. "Pass the word, B Team personnel proceed independently as instructed. They must arrive here no later than fifteen hundred hours day after tomorrow."

As Contabile relayed the message, Mr. Molto turned to the other young man. "Put the following cities on Special B Team Alert, and I want confirmation within three hours that they are ready to accommodate us: food, lodging, transport, weapons and munitions, troops."

Molto paused, then said, "Dallas-Fort Worth, Detroit, Seattle, Toronto-Montreal."

"Yes, sir," the young man said and read the list back verbatim. Molto nodded and left the CIC by the elevator. Back in his bedroom, he stripped off and got into the shower.

As he lathered, Mr. Molto thought, Seattle. All the other was a shuck. I can't let them know it's that easy. It took me long enough to sell the old bastards on the idea, so I'll make it look tough, and make them spend money, wasted money. That's how you make people believe in you. They place the value on you that you place upon yourself. The more this operation costs, the better they believe it is, now that I finally sold them. Bolan's a goddam soldier, a real professional fighting man. He thinks like a professional fighting man, and he operates the same way. You don't take a guy like that down with 1930 gangster movie methods.

With contempt, Mr. Molto thought of the Taliferi, the Lord High Chief Enforcers of *La Cosa Nostra*. Every time those bigshots went after Bolan he humilated them, killed the two brothers, sent their "secret weapon's" head back to them in a sack. Wild Card. My ass!

Well, buddy-boy bastard Bolan, measure your life expectancy in hours. You've got another soldier fighting you now, and I'm not only a better man personally, I'm smarter, more experienced, a lifetime of soldiering compared to your ten lousy years, and I've got unlimited financial and manpower resources. Check it in buddy-boy, because I've read your mind. I'll meet you in Seattle, sweetheart, and blow your ass up before you get one good breath of Puget Sound air!

Almost halfway around the world, Mack Bolan stirred and woke for a moment, trying to remember the disquieting dream that seemed to have taken his breath. He could remember nothing, and decided that the pain had waked him. He thought about the information Donato passed on. He would have to verify it, call on Leo Turrin again, but if half what Donato said was true, Seattle needed a Bolan blitz, a visit with The Executioner!

PINNACLE
BOOKS

THE INCREDIBLE, ACTION-PACKED SERIES

DEATH MERCHANT

His name is Richard Camellion; he's a master of disguise, deception and destruction. He does what the CIA and FBI cannot do. They call him THE DEATH MERCHANT!

Order		Title	Book No.	Price
_____	#1	The Death Merchant	PO21N	95c
_____	#2	Operation Overkill	PO85N	95c
_____	#3	The Psychotron Plot	P117N	95c
_____	#4	Chinese Conspiracy	P168N	95c
_____	#5	Satan Strike	P166N	95¢
			and more to come . . .